Mills & Boon Best Seller Romance

A chance to read and collect some of the best-loved novels from Mills & Boon—the world's largest publisher of romantic fiction.

Every month, six titles by favourite Mills & Boon authors will be re-published in the *Best Seller Romance* series.

A list of other titles in the *Best Seller Romance* series can be found at the end of this book.

Mary Wibberley

THE SNOW ON THE HILLS

MILLS & BOON LIMITED
LONDON · TORONTO

All the characters in this book have no existence outside the imagination of the Author, and have no relation whatsoever to anyone bearing the same name or names. They are not even distantly inspired by any individual known or unknown to the Author, and all the incidents are pure invention.

The text of this publication or any part thereof may not be reproduced or transmitted in any form or by any means, electronic or mechanical, including photocopying, recording, storage in an information retrieval system, or otherwise, without the written permission of the publisher.

This book is sold subject to the condition that it shall not, by way of trade or otherwise, be lent, resold, hired out or otherwise circulated without the prior consent of the publisher in any form of binding or cover other than that in which it is published and without a similar condition including this condition being imposed on the subsequent purchaser.

First published 1974
Australian copyright 1982
Philippine copyright 1982
This edition 1982

© *Mary Wibberley 1974*

ISBN 0 263 74138 9

Set in Linotype Plantin 11 on 12½ pt.
02–1282

Made and printed in Great Britain by
Richard Clay (The Chaucer Press) Ltd,
Bungay, Suffolk

CHAPTER ONE

VANESSA dropped the sugar cube into her coffee and watched the bubbles rise. It wasn't her imagination; the two youths in motor-cycle gear were eyeing her with unconcealed interest.

She was used to it. But this was slightly different. Their looks were making her feel uncomfortable. The café was small. Two girls behind the counter, giggling as they whispered together, a man sitting in the corner drinking coffee – and the two youths. They had finished their toast. They were making two Cokes spin out a ridiculous time.

Vanessa looked at the man who seemed more interested in the newspaper beside him on the table than anything else. And what could she say if she did go up to him? 'Will you tell those two youths to stop staring at me?' He would probably look at her as if she was mad. But she was uneasy. The next stretch of road was lonely, she already knew that from her map – and from what had gone before. Thirty miles from Deanston House, thirty miles of bleak Highlands to drive through before she reached her goal, and little traffic anywhere.

The man glanced up briefly, as if sensing her eyes on him, looked first at the youths, then down to his paper again. Vanessa's heart skipped a beat. There would be no help there. Perhaps he thought she actually liked it! They were now making little noises with their lips pursed, like calling a cat, and laughing quietly. The coffee tasted awful.

She stood up. Time to go – the sooner the better. Her head already ached from the long drive since Perth, and what was to come at Deanston House – the unknown place – when she eventually arrived. The quicker she was on her way the better it would be. She picked up her jacket and handbag and went out without once looking back.

Outside it was cool, with a hint of rain in the sky. Towering hills were bleak in the evening light, and everything was quiet. Two motor-cycles stood at one side of the café car park, and a sleek maroon Jaguar – and Vanessa's own grey Cortina. She slid in, flung her coat and bag on the front passenger seat and started the engine. Somehow, in her mind was the thought that if she could only get going before they came out, all would be well . . .

And then, as she moved into the road, she saw the café door open, and they stood there on the step for a moment, sharply outlined against the lighted background. They were laughing again. Instinctively she leaned over and banged the buttons down to lock all the doors. Then she pressed her foot down hard on the accelerator, and the Cortina responded instantly.

She drove down the road as fast as she dared. But perhaps that would not be fast enough. Those motor-bikes were powerful, for all their comic appearance with the ridiculously raised handlebars, dozen or so mirrors set at all angles, and imitation tiger tails hanging from what looked like radio aerials at the back. They roared after her, and she knew fear – and an odd feeling that this could be a punishment for the deliberate deception on which she was about to embark.

But now was not the time for soul-searching. Now it

was important for her to keep ahead, just to keep in front and it would be all right. The road stretched out, a grey asphalt ribbon, and vanished as it curved, and Vanessa followed it, and her hands were damp on the wheel. She was not a nervous person, was in fact usually well controlled. But there had been *something* in the glances of those two youths – surely neither more than twenty – that had made her feel slightly sick.

A sudden jolting memory of the other customer in the small café came irresistibly back to her. He had been attractive, in a hard, almost grim way, and— And then the roar came behind her. The curve had hidden them. Now they were visible – and menacing. Two young men, out for kicks, dressed in studded black leather jackets and tight jeans. And they were nearer. And where, oh, where was there another car, or a lorry – *anything*?

The wind as the first passed her almost vibrated the car. Their methods weren't subtle, but highly effective. Number One waited until she was at a passing place and slewed across the road ahead of her so that she instinctively put the brake on. The second was behind her, effectively blocking any thoughts of reversing. Vanessa had the wild urge to press the accelerator and drive on – but she knew it would be no use. The powerful bike was too big to run over, and the road wasn't wide enough to pass it. And then silence fell as all engines stopped.

She looked round desperately for a weapon. Her handbag – fingers feverishly scrabbling – then cool roundness – a perfume spray. Small enough, but better than nothing. And how long before they forced the doors open?

Number One leaned down and rapped the window –

and grinned. His teeth were bad, his face spotty. But his eyes held a knowledge beyond his years.

'Please go away.' Stupid words to say, and they came out almost like a prayer.

And then – unbelievably – there came a long blast of a horn from behind them. Vanessa turned, her heart leaping to her throat in sudden relief. Now! It was now or never. And she saw the Jaguar that had been at the café – the dark man's – and he was blasting his horn because Number One's bike was blocking his way. She fumbled for the catch and pushed the door open even as the youth went to move his motor-cycle. *He* wanted no interference. Let the Jaguar pass. She had only seconds. But then, even as she stumbled out, ignoring the second one's outstretched, *impertinent* arm – the Jaguar driver got out, slamming his door shut behind him, and Vanessa tried to still the trembling of her legs as he walked slowly towards her car.

'Please help me,' she said. 'These two—'

'I know. I saw them.' He had a deep voice. Perhaps it was pleasant normally, but now he seemed angry – almost scornful. That much struck Vanessa as she looked at him, seeing only a method of salvation. At first, that is. And then she realized something, and the fear came back. He was one, they were two – and tough. He didn't look particularly tough. Although he was tall and broad-shouldered, he had an indolent, casual way of walking. She had noticed that even as he had come into the café when she was half-way through her sandwiches – and the youths hadn't yet begun pestering her. He looked like a man who would prefer to walk away from trouble. But he wouldn't, would he? He wouldn't just leave her?

8

Then he spoke. Number One had moved his motorcycle to one side – enough for the Jaguar to pass – but even nearer Vanessa's car. So that . . .

'On your way, lads,' he said, and he smiled.

Number One, the undoubted leader, stood where he was, legs slightly apart, hands on hips in an arrogant stance. 'Listen, I've just moved my bike, okay?' he answered, in accents from darkest Glasgow, barely comprehensible. 'So why don't you get on *your* way? We're not bothering you.'

'No,' the dark man conceded. 'But this young lady objects to you stopping her, and I don't blame her. So—' But he wasn't allowed to finish.

Vanessa had half turned, because the second one was too quiet, so she saw him first, and began: 'Look out—' but the warning was unnecessary. The second one had a bottle in his hand. And if it had connected with its target, the dark man would have gone to the ground. But it didn't. She watched in horrified fascination as he reached out to grasp the youth's wrist, to twist – and then he seemed to turn his own body, so casually. It was fascinating to watch, because everything had an almost electric, slow-motion quality to it, seeing the youth's face, the expression of surprise as the bottle dropped out of nerveless fingers, seeing him follow it to the ground – and then Number One hurled himself forward, and Vanessa thought: This is it, and looked round her for a stone or a stick – for anything to help . . .

It all happened too quickly for her even to have reached anything, even if she could. Number One came at a rush towards the dark man, his hands up to get the other's face, and there was power behind that run because he was a hefty youth, broadly built, and strong with it. And it was strange, almost frightening to see him go over the other man, who seemed to fall backward, and was then *on top* of Number One, quite suddenly and easily.

Judo! Vanessa knew then. Of course. But how different when seen on television, with opponents neatly dressed in white jacket and trousers, from this – this *reality*!

It was all over. The Jaguar driver stood and brushed his jacket, looking down dispassionately at the two figures trying groggily to climb to their feet. Then he turned to Vanessa. 'Get in your car,' he said. 'Drive on – I'll follow. Quickly now!'

There was no time to talk. Wordlessly she obeyed, hands trembling a little as she switched on the ignition, then steadying as she realized that if anyone should be shaking, it was the Jaguar driver, not her.

Five miles later, by a passing place, the Jaguar's lights went on, signalling her to stop, and she did so, then quickly got out. The first thing she had to do was to thank him . . .

He was striding over – and he gave her no chance. 'What's your name?' he demanded, most disconcertingly. Vanessa's little speech of thanks died unspoken.

'Vanessa—' she began – and *couldn't remember* her new surname. 'Er – Smith.'

One eyebrow lifted, faintly cynical. 'You seem to have a job remembering it.'

Her dark eyes flashed briefly with temper. 'I'm confused – I had a fright.'

'Yes,' he nodded. 'Well, Miss *Smith*—' Did he hesitate slightly before that word? – 'I don't advise you to travel alone in future – not in lonely places like this, anyway. If no one had come, you'd have been in dead trouble, you know that?'

Her gratitude was rapidly being swept away by his arrogant manner, but she clung on to the last vestiges sufficiently well to enable her to say: 'Yes, and I appreciate what you did very much.'

'I knew in the café what they were up to. I'd have followed even if I hadn't been coming this way anyway.'

'Oh!' He really was having the oddest effect on her. Rarely was she lost for words. Rarely too did a man seem so frightfully *immune*, almost as if he was not really seeing her at all. He was tall too, which was rather annoying, for being five foot eight, Vanessa was not really used to having to look up to speak to anyone. But with him, she did, which put her at a distinct disadvantage, for he *knew*. He was over six feet by several inches, broad-shouldered with it, tanned face, most unusual green eyes that seemed almost – no, they couldn't be – *mocking* her.

'So either have company on your travels, or learn karate or something,' he finished.

'I'm going to take up a post thirty miles away,' she answered, snapping back a retort that would have been almost rude. 'I could hardly fetch my nanny with me, could I? As for karate, I've always considered the Highlands to be a respectable, *safe* place for the traveller – and the Scots most hospitable – but I'll have a rethink about that, Mr. – er—?' For he had a faint Scots accent, and let him take that how he chose. Vanessa's temper was on the rise, and the sooner she was away, the better.

'Cal Grayne, Miss *Smith*.' There was no imagining the emphasis on the word this time.

'Hadn't we better be going?' she said, and half moved away. 'Those two—'

'Will be looking for their keys in the heather for quite a while yet.' He smiled. Nothing humorous, a mere grin, but he had good teeth. 'And even if they find them, they'd be sorry if they tried to follow us. They'd not force *me* to stop.' It wasn't boasting, just a statement of fact.

Vanessa couldn't prevent the words. 'It must be *nice* to be so sure of yourself,' and she smiled too, and she knew the effect that smile could have on men. It always knocked them for six. But not him.

'Yes, it is.' And he looked down on her. 'And you have a fine little temper, haven't you, miss? Perhaps you'd rather I'd let them clonk me with the bottle?'

'I didn't mean that!' She was beginning to feel confused. Who the hell did he think he was? Arrogant beast! 'I meant—' but she wasn't sure what she *did* mean now. She finished lamely. 'You seem to think it was all my fault.'

He looked at her, and the expression on that darkly attractive face was most strange, just for a moment. 'Has nobody ever taught you to keep your eyes to yourself – when you're in certain company?'

'What!' He surely didn't think ... 'How *dare* you! What are you implying?' Her beautiful oval face was normally pale, so fair was her skin in contrast to her black hair, but now her cheeks were pink, and her dark brown eyes flashed dangerously.

'Oh, come *on*!' He spoke patiently, almost as if to a child. 'Don't tell me you didn't give them the slightest encouragement – not intentionally—' he raised a hand as he said the last two words, placatingly, as if knowing her thoughts, '—but you can't help it, can you? You know you're attractive – you'd be a fool, or a liar, if you said you didn't – and you should have known you could cause trouble just by—'

'I'm not staying to listen to *you*, Mr. Grayne,' she breathed, and swung away to go back to her car. 'I'm not sure who's worse. Good-bye!'

There was silence. He neither spoke, nor made any move to stop her. And what had she expected?

As she drove off down the road she looked into her rear view mirror. He was just getting into his car, long-legged, sliding in easily. Not looking at her, not remotely interested. Vanessa compressed her lips. He was quite hateful – even if he had saved her from something very unpleasant. She looked round again before a bend in the road hid his car from view. The glow of a cigarette came faintly from the windscreen, and her heart contracted. Could he be waiting, just to make sure there was no more trouble? It was possible. But now as she drove along, there came more pressing thoughts into Vanessa's mind. Thoughts of where exactly she was going – and the reason why.

A very strange thing happened when she was only a few miles away from Deanston House. She had stopped to read the map, and to confirm the turn off which loomed sharply to the right, a road leading into apparently impenetrable bleak mountain. She must be *sure*, before she went, for there might be nowhere to turn round for several miles, and it was growing rapidly darker, with rain-swollen clouds sweeping lower every minute.

It was. She had marked the map carefully at the solicitor's office, following his instructions, and there was no mistaking that twisty angle which the road took. Vanessa stuck the map in the glove compartment and checking that the road was clear both ways, turned right. Dimly, almost invisible in the distance, a vehicle of some kind travelled at speed along the road she had just left, and for a brief moment she wondered if it could be the Jaguar. Unlikely, but possible. Then she was too busy negotiating a high narrow bend to worry about arrogant knight errants ... Until the next minute he was behind her, following her up the road.

She looked through her mirror, frowning, disbelieving ... But there was no mistaking the car – or the face behind the wheel. The face that even now she could see bore an expression of hard incredulity.

It was no use. Vanessa could hardly make him wait while she negotiated the unfamiliar twists of the road – but surely it led only to Deanston House? But could he still be following her? Did he perhaps want to tell her something? She waved him on at the next passing place, a mere widening of the road surface indicated by the usual white pole and diamond-shaped sign. He stopped instead of passing, and she had no choice but to do the same.

She wound down her window. What on earth could he want?

'Look, are you on the right road?' His deep voice was quite impersonal. The scenes between them might never have been.

'Yes. I thought you wanted to ask me something. I'm going to a place called Deanston House—' and she stopped abruptly at the expression on his face, the sudden shocked awareness. 'What is it?' she faltered. What had she said?

'*You're* going to Deanston?' he demanded. 'Don't tell me *you're* the one who's coming to catalogue the library? My God!'

It was those last two words that did it. Vanessa pushed at the door, he moved slightly aside, opening it for her as he did so; she stepped out.

'Look,' she said, 'I've just about had enough – I don't know who or what you are, but it's no business of yours *where* I'm going. Just because you "saved" me from those two—'

She wasn't allowed to finish. He was looking at her with something like amused contempt on his face. 'Hold that temper,' he interrupted, voice as rock-hard as his face. 'It'll get you nowhere with me. And it won't do your looks any good either—'

'Why, you—!'

'See what I mean? Eyes flashing fire, cheeks red – calm down, little Miss Wildcat, and *listen*.'

Vanessa's breast heaved as she fought for control against the most maddeningly *arrogant* creature she had ever met. How she would like to slap that lean hard face!

'That's better.' He would never know how close he had been ... 'I've got every right to ask if you're going to Deanston – especially as I happen to be staying there myself.'

For a moment Vanessa just looked at him. It wasn't possible. It just was not possible – was it? In a rather smaller voice she said:

'It belongs to a Mr. Maclean, and as far as I know he lives—'

'Alone,' he finished smoothly. 'Yes, in a sense he does, except for the staff looking after him. But at the moment I'm his – guest.' There had been the faintest, imperceptible pause before that last word, but she scarcely noticed it in her dismay. She could have done without this complication. She looked at him. She must be very careful, she knew. Too much was happening too suddenly. She must be calm. It would give her time to think. And she was beginning to realize that time for reflection would be a luxury she could ill afford – yet.

'I see,' she said, and smiled at him, her best, most seductive smile – and he reacted – but only momentarily, so fleetingly that she knew she had imagined it when his next words came.

'And of course I was surprised because I had imagined the new – er – employee's name to be—' he paused, and clicked his fingers as if searching his memory, '—Miss Collins.' And he stopped. He smiled slowly at Vanessa, and the smile said it for him: 'Get out of *that*.'

Those few seconds had prepared her, had given her the vital time to think. 'That's right,' she agreed. 'When I told you my name was Smith before, it was simply a – a natural reluctance to tell my name to a stranger.'

One dark eyebrow lifted fractionally. That wide mouth quirked. 'Ah yes, of course,' he agreed softly. 'And I don't blame you. There are certainly some odd types hanging out around here just lately. Very wise.' But she knew with a stone cold certainty that he didn't believe her. The main thing was – would it matter?

When, minutes later, she found herself following him meekly along the twisting road that seemed to grow narrower by the yard, Vanessa allowed her tired brain to contemplate the problem. He drove the Jaguar slowly, as if in consideration for her unfamiliarity. Slowly and skilfully, and in such a way that she was confident to follow him exactly.

So he was a guest in Deanston House. For how long? She frowned slightly. And the scene in Mr. Murton's office came back to her with a startling clarity that she wasn't sure she was ready for. She knew she would have to think about it – but not yet. Not just yet . . . But the image persisted, of Mr. Murton's worried face, his gentle voice mildly reproving:

'But I cannot condone deception of any sort—'

'I'm not asking you to condone anything,' Vanessa could even remember her own voice as it had been, logical, practical, *determined* to batter any resistance – because she had already made up her mind.

'But it seems to me—' Mr. Murton picked up a sheaf of papers, 'as if you're going to go there and pretend to be someone else—'

'I've already explained that,' she said, and smiled slowly at him. He never had been able to resist Vanessa's smile. She heard his confused cough as she went on: 'It's only for a little while, a week or so, then I'll tell him. It's like a – a game.' And God forgive me for the lies, she added inwardly. But no one must know her true reason, the desire to see this old man who had ruined her father's life – Andrew Maclean, her grandfather, who had just spent thousands trying to trace the only child of his recently dead son.

She was brought back to the present by the slowing down of the Jaguar, and she instinctively applied her brakes. It was a sheep that had strayed from the hillside.

It lumbered away, clumsy with wool, slightly indignant at having a mid-road nap interrupted, and the man imperceptibly increased his speed, followed in turn by Vanessa. She looked in her rear view mirror for a moment. Her eyes were large and dark, and she wondered if she was wrong after all, wrong to come here. Her father now – would he have condoned what she was doing? She would never really know. Mr. Murton had been terribly uneasy, that was obvious. But she had given him no choice. He had made the mistake of telling her that he had also been asked if he would find a suitable person – man or woman – to catalogue the library at Deanston House.

'You've found her,' Vanessa had answered, a great wave of relief surging through her. 'Don't you see? I'll do it. You can tell them you know of someone, and—'

'And what when you reveal your true identity?' Mr. Murton interrupted dryly. 'How does that make me look? A fellow conspirator?'

'No.' Vanessa had stood up then. 'Because I've told you – and you know I mean it – that if you tell my – my grandfather—' she nearly choked over the word, 'that you've found me, and where I live, I'll go away immediately, and I'll make sure he never finds me – ever.'

The elderly solicitor had been torn. She had felt sorry for him. But the desire for revenge was infinitely more powerful. And she knew she had won.

She was now Vanessa Collins, with a new, well rehearsed background and life story to tell if anyone asked. She was going to see the place where her father had been born and spent his childhood years, and she was going to see the man she had heard so many bitter, unforgiving words about, and she was going to make him like her and then tell him who she was, and watch his face, and then walk out of the house, away from there, never to return. Then she would know peace of mind for the first time in two years, ever since her father, on his sickbed, had told her the story of the harsh, hard man who had thrown him out because he had wanted to marry the wrong girl, and not the one Andrew Maclean had chosen. And now they were both dead, her mother and father, her mother of a broken heart soon after her husband, and it was all her grandfather's fault ...

She saw the man ahead of her signalling to turn right, into dense woodland, and she followed. This one had managed to throw her, when he had asked her name. Just for a few vital seconds she had forgotten who she was supposed to be – and that must not be allowed to happen again. She would watch Cal Grayne, this dark powerful man who gave her the disconcerting impression that he could read her thoughts – almost.

The road was a narrow one, the trees high and proud, shadowing everything in an eerie dark light that would never alter. And what would she find? She hadn't even got any photographs of Deanston House to prepare her. Her father had destroyed anything that might serve as a reminder of what had once been. She had no idea either what her grandfather might look like – but she had a mental picture, and it wasn't a pleasant one. Soon she would see for herself, and the imaginings, and the speculation would all be over.

Into a gateway, white posts, wrought iron gates well back, the drive rough and stony at first and rhododendrons banked, seeming to go on for ever, at each side of the road. Cal Grayne blasted his horn briefly, and she wondered if it was a signal to someone, then saw the young rabbits dart away from their perilous, centre-of-the-drive play area. Her lips curved faintly. At least he didn't like running over animals. A slight point in his favour, but only slight. She didn't like him – and the feeling was mutual, his manner had made that clear already. He was very shrewd, she imagined. No good him discovering her identity, and spoiling her plan. She would have to treat him with great caution, she decided, there and then. And in another few weeks, when the time came, it wouldn't matter any more.

Then she saw the house, and her heart contracted in a strange kind of sudden sadness. So this had been her father's home. And it was beautiful, so very beautiful – an immense grey stone building, with high arched windows and huge portico dominating the front. Wide steps led up to the door, and the porch was shadowed and dark, and as they stopped a sudden flash of lightning lit the house in a blur of blue-white colour.

Just for an instant of time, but it seemed like an omen. Vanessa switched off her engine, and her car settled into silence, and then distantly came the thunder, and she had the absurd desire to turn and drive away...

'Let's get in.' Her door was opened, shattering her thoughts into tiny fragments. 'It's going to pour down in a minute. Where's your luggage?'

'In the boot.' She removed her keys from the ignition and began to get out. He took the keys from her, walked round the back and unlocked the boot and lifted out her two cases. Vanessa was torn between the desire to thank him, and indignation at the cool way he had taken her keys. Almost as if he was rapidly losing patience with her, and couldn't even be bothered to explain his actions. Leaning in the car, she lifted her jacket and bag from the seat. Instinct told her to let his high-handedness pass. For now, anyway.

He led the way up the worn stone steps and pushed open a huge front door, the top half of which was of stained glass.

'Welcome to Deanston House, Miss Collins,' he said, and it was very difficult to tell exactly what was in his voice – but it wasn't welcome, that was sure.

'Thank you, Mr. Grayne.' She smiled at him. The masquerade had begun. Too late to turn back now. It must be carried off with whatever effort it cost her. She shook her head slightly to move her dark heavy tresses away from her face, and asked: 'What do I do now?'

'Why, I'll show you to your room,' he said. 'And I dare say you'll unpack. And then we'll have dinner.'

'Hadn't I better meet Mr. Maclean before I go up?'

He cocked a dark eyebrow. 'Didn't I say? He's away tonight. Back tomorrow lunch, I think. Until then I'll look after you.' And the words had a faintly sinister ring to them. All her imagination, of course, but she felt an uneasy twinge.

'And if I hadn't happened to meet you?' she inquired softly.

'The housekeeper and her husband are here, the Banks. She would have fed you and shown you round.' He picked up her cases and walked towards the stairs which dominated the huge hall. They led up to a half landing with stained glass windows, mainly shades of amber and gold, and then branched to either side upwards. As Vanessa walked up beside the dark man carrying her luggage, a flash of lightning lit up the window, and the effect was eerie, almost frightening. Perhaps she flinched, for she almost glimpsed his grin before it vanished. 'Scared of storms?' he asked, almost sympathetically — only it wasn't genuine, he was more amused than concerned.

'Not at all,' she answered. 'Are you?'

He laughed. 'I have a healthy respect for lightning,' he said. 'I've seen what it can do. But no, I'm not frightened.'

'You'd hardly admit it if you were,' Vanessa answered, swiftly and sweetly. 'I mean, are you frightened of *anything*?'

They were at the top of the stairs now, on another large landing, thickly and richly carpeted, with two wide corridors leading away at either side, and Cal Grayne stopped and put her cases down, the movements slow and deliberate.

'You know,' he remarked almost conversationally, 'we're going to have to get on together if you intend staying here a while. If I were you I'd watch that tongue of yours. For such a young woman it's uncommonly sharp.'

She felt as if he had slapped her. With a great effort she managed to answer him fairly calmly. 'Are you threatening me?'

'Why, no!' he seemed faintly surprised. 'Just commenting. Do I look as though I would threaten a woman?' The mockery was veiled, but it was there all right.

'I don't know you well enough to say,' she shot back quickly. 'Nor do I particularly want to. But you can be remarkably rude without even trying. You were before, after you had rescued me. You implied—' she had to falter – 'you implied that I'd been encouraging those disgusting youths—'

'I didn't,' he cut in. 'I merely suggested you'd do better to keep those flashing eyes to yourself when you were in certain company—'

'As though I'd been m-making eyes at them or something,' she retorted. It was strange, standing there on a shadowy landing, for all she knew the only two people in a vast mansion, arguing with this complete stranger, feeling the need – the *urge* – to just once get the better of him. She took a deep breath, to help her get control. And he laughed. He *laughed*.

'Well, weren't you?' he asked.

Vanessa launched herself at him, her hand going up to wipe that grin off his detestable face. 'How—' she began, but that was as far as she got.

She was caught and held with no apparent effort, and he looked down at her, and his eyes gleamed darkly in that dim light, and the grip on her arms was cool and inflexible.

'Little wildcat, aren't you?' he remarked. 'What a hell of a temper you've got. You know, I might just tame you—'

'Let me go!' she breathed.

'When I'm ready, and not before. You'll listen to me for a minute, now I've got you just where I want you—' Vanessa tried to wrench herself free, but the grip tightened imperceptibly.

'You're hurting me,' she said, breathing hard. It was horrible to feel helpless, so completely helpless. How she hated him! How *dare* he!

'Then stand still. I'm not letting you slap my face,

and you will if I let your arms go, so until you cool down, you're stopping like that.'

'If you don't let me go at once, I shall kick you hard,' she said – and she meant it.

'Try it,' he answered, voice as soft as a whisper – and as sharp as tempered steel. 'Just try it. Once. And I promise you you'll not be tempted again in a hurry.'

The icy shock of his words stilled her, and she felt a fine tremor run through her body. What would he do? And she remembered the two youths from the café, and the way he had so quietly, almost effortlessly dealt with them, and she was afraid. Without realizing it, she allowed her body to relax. Better, she thought, not to resist him any more. Not to give him the chance to try any judo throws on *her* . . .

'That's better. You've stopped resisting.' The hold on her arms loosened, and Cal Grayne's face became less hard. 'Just so long as you always remember – you can't fight me – so don't try.'

'You're loathesome,' she whispered. 'Are you going to let me go?'

'Are you going to hit me?'

'No.'

The pressure was off. She rubbed her arms where his fingers had rested, and looked down at her cases. She didn't even have the strength to pick them up. For some reason her arms felt as weak as a child's almost as if the muscles had gone on strike. 'What have you done to me?' she asked. 'I can hardly—'

'Nothing. And if you're so weak and helpless I suggest you learn how to defend yourself against attack. Then the next time two yobboes decide to follow you, you may be able to take *them* by surprise.'

'I must remember to book judo lessons when I get back to London,' she said sarcastically.

He looked shrewdly, assessingly at her. 'No need to wait. You can start now – I'll teach you. It'll be a pleasure.' And he grinned. Vanessa didn't know how to take that grin – or his words. She looked coldly at him.

'May we go to my room now?' she asked. 'I'd like to wash and change.'

'Of course. This way.' He picked up her cases and strode off. As she followed that broad retreating back, she thought of what he had just said.

As if she would let him teach her anything! As if she would – but then came the thought, unbidden, fleeting: It *could* be interesting. The thought was very quickly banished.

CHAPTER TWO

VANESSA had a shock when she first saw her room. She hid it well until Cal Grayne had gone, for she wouldn't give him the satisfaction of seeing her stunned surprise.

The room was enormous, high-ceilinged, and quite beautiful. It was at the front of the house, and had two big bay windows that looked out on breathtaking views of the gardens through which they had so recently driven. She crossed over to see out better, and stood quite still, reaching out to touch the heavy green velvet curtains that waited to be drawn together when night fell. It was growing rapidly darker, even as she looked, and thunder growled and rumbled round the sky, as if the storm was moving away. Rain started as she watched, heavy grey sheets sweeping down to earth, and the light had a strange green tinge to it that was eerie. Vanessa turned away to look around the room, seeing the fitted furniture, all of good rich dark wood, the greeny-grey autumn-coloured carpet that stretched thickly around her. There were two big easy chairs, her bed with its candlewick cover in cream, patterned with roses. A grandfather clock stood in one corner, and a huge vase was on a table, both of which looked fragile – and valuable. There was even a television set in the corner by the window.

Everything had the rich gleam of being cared for, and she had a sudden twinge of guilt, which she quickly suppressed. It was no good feeling like this when she had only been here five minutes. The decision was taken, and she would go through with it. She would – for her father's sake.

Vanessa put her hand to her eyes, feeling a sudden pain, the sharp anguish of knowing, whatever she did, that it was too late to really do anything, now. Much too late. She took a deep breath and crossed the room to a mirrored door near her bed, wondering if it was to a built-in wardrobe. She opened it – and was in a bathroom! No wonder Cal Grayne had not bothered to tell her where one was! She had assumed he was doing it merely to annoy her – to make her ask. But it had probably not occurred to him at all.

It was small and compact, the walls mirror-covered, and its bay window, at the side of the house, overlooking dense woodland. She looked round her and sighed softly. How different it all could have been, if only . . . But it was no use thinking like that. Vanessa determinedly went out and shut the door. She would unpack and put her clothes away, then have a good wash and change.

The lights made the room seem warmer and smaller, for they were soft, gold-shaded, and cleverly placed. Vanessa drew the curtains together with a long soothing swish, unlocked her cases, and began to unpack.

The hall was silent when she went downstairs, silent save for the ponderous chimes of a huge clock in the corner. A standard lamp had been lit and it cast a warm orange glow over the panelled walls, the monk's bench, and polished cabinet in the rather sombre hall. The storm had completely passed over, only the rain came down, drumming steadily against the windows behind her on the half landing, and on an impulse she went to the front door and opened it to look out at the grey blur that was now the gardens. She shivered slightly, feeling cold, and a voice from behind her said: 'Not thinking of going for a walk?'

Slowly she turned. She knew who it was, of course. She had never heard anyone with a voice quite like his, very deep, always with that hidden touch of insolent amusement — at least when addressing her, as if he found her funny — and that was annoying, but she wouldn't show it.

'I was just looking,' she answered. The memory of their last brief skirmish lingered, and her arms still tingled at the touch of his strong hands. And she knew she was going to have to be very careful with Mr. Cal Grayne, now and in the future. He had changed into a very comfortable-looking suit of fawn suede jacket and matching pants, and a pink open-necked shirt. And he was, she realized with a sudden pang — almost of dismay — extremely attractive, for the jacket emphasized the powerful shoulders and build of him, and she wondered why she had thought he would be a man to walk away from trouble at that first meeting. He looked assured, confident — and completely relaxed. A dismaying combination for Vanessa, the newcomer, to face. She looked quickly down at herself, relieved that she too had changed, into a smart blue and white check trouser suit in which she always felt terrific. She was tall and slender, with a neat bosom and long slim legs, and the crisp white blouse she wore with the suit emphasized the delicate colouring of her face. She *knew* she looked good — and how she needed a prop to her confidence — with *him*!

'Are you hungry?' he asked. 'Mrs. Banks wants to know.'

'Yes, I am. But I don't want to put her to any—'

'You won't,' he cut in shortly. 'She has it ready.'

'Tell me,' Vanessa said sweetly, knowing that she shouldn't, yet unable to resist, because he was quite the *rudest* man, 'do you ever let anyone finish a sentence?'

He laughed. 'I haven't time to listen to people waffling on, if that's what you mean. I believe in getting to the point.'

'Oh yes,' she agreed, and nodded. 'Don't you just! I must remember that. See how *you* like being interrupted in mid-sentence.'

Cal cocked an amused eyebrow. 'It must be hunger that's making you bad-tempered,' and his tone was deceptively mild. 'Come on, I'll take you to the dining-room. You'll feel better when you've eaten.' And he touched her arm lightly.

Vanessa shook it free. 'I'm not a child – thank you,' she said. 'If you lead the way, I'll follow.'

He shut the door with a quiet snick. 'All right,' he said. 'This way.' He strode off to the right of the hall, down a corridor, past several closed doors, and into a vast room with a long table large enough to seat two dozen people. Her heart sank. She was going to eat – *here*! A tray in her room seemed the most delightful prospect at that moment. But there was worse to come. There were two places set at one end of the table. Two. She looked at him.

'Oh!' she said.

'Oh, yes.' And he smiled. His teeth were good and strong and white, she noticed inconsequently. 'I couldn't let you eat alone in this—' he waved one arm expansively, '—could I?'

'Couldn't you? I thought it would appeal to you,' she answered, uncaring now.

'I'm your host, remember? Until Mr. Maclean returns,' and there was a hint of menace in that smooth deep voice. It warned her. Taking a deep breath, she managed to say, with great coolness:

'Which one shall I have?'

He pulled out the chair at her nearside, and gestured. 'If you'd like to sit down?'

The next minute a woman came in pushing a trolley, a small hatchet-faced body with short grey hair, dressed severely in black. She looked hard at Vanessa before saying to Cal: 'Here's the soup. It's better drunk nice and hot, as you know.'

'Indeed I do.' He smiled at her, quite charmingly, Vanessa noted with surprise. 'And this is Vanessa Collins, Mrs. Banks, the young lady who's come to do the library.'

Mrs. Banks nodded, and the slight compression of her lips was probably meant to be a smile. 'Hmm, good. Fed up of the dirty books I am.' She looked again at Vanessa, a hard shrewd glance, before putting the plates on the table and going out. Her accent, Vanessa realized in some surprise, had been purest Cockney.

The soup was a rich thick homemade tomato, and was quite delicious. Cal had waited for her to begin before he picked up his own spoon. 'Her bark's worse than her bite,' he observed dryly, as if sensing Vanessa's surprise. 'And just to clarify a point, when she said "dirty" books, she meant the state of them, not the content.'

'Of course,' she lifted a delicate brow in pretended amazement. He wasn't the only one who could put on an air of astonishment. 'I didn't imagine otherwise.' And she bent to her soup.

Mrs. Banks had also brought in crusty rolls. Vanessa took one and broke it in half. It was freshly baked, still warm, and the unmistakable smell of new bread. And she was starving. She had not realized just how hungry before. She decided that she wasn't going to let Cal Grayne spoil her meal, whatever he said. To give him his due he seemed too busy himself even to look at her. She was able, very discreetly, to observe him as he bent to his soup, the light overhead from ornate chandeliers casting golden light on his dark hair, turning it to fire. There was something very strong about that face. Vanessa couldn't think why she had thought him not tough before. First appearances could be deceptive, and his had been. The way he had dealt with the two youths had soon established that fact. Then something else came to her, a disturbing thought. Not only had he not been frightened of them, he had seemed almost to be enjoying himself. She bent to her plate to hide a flare of dismay. For upstairs on the landing, before, she had been aware of the disturbing sensation again. And what chance would she stand against a man like him? He had threatened her, actually threatened her, when she had told him she would kick him. Maybe he had the right. But – more than that – she had felt a cold tingle along her spine; a tingle of apprehension and something else besides that she could not define, but which had caused her heart to beat faster. Whatever happened now, she had beeen warned. She must try not to tangle with him – ever. But even as she had the thought, there came another, more disturbing; how difficult would that be?

'And this is the conservatory.' Cal Grayne was showing Vanessa round the house, his air of mocking amusement never far away, yet his manner with nothing at all that she could fault about it.

Their voices had a faint echo as they entered the large damp-aired glass-roofed building. It was warm but humid, and she shivered slightly, looking round her at exotic plants and succulents growing in tubs and pots, and even a gnarled old vine stretching up and all over the glass roof. She looked up, caught a glimpse of deep purple grapes hidden in the leaves, felt the moisture all about them, and said faintly: 'It's fascinating.'

'Yes, isn't it?' he agreed. 'I thought you'd like it here.' Not enough in his tone for sarcasm, but it was there, well veiled. Oh, hateful man! She looked at him. She would keep her temper, she *would*, because if she lost it—

'I'd like to see the library,' she said nicely. 'You are going to show me, aren't you?' The meal had been delicious, if slowly served, and they were going to have coffee afterwards in the lounge, but first Cal had insisted on showing her round.

'Of course. That next, as a matter of fact.' He had taken her round, showing her the lounge, a brief glimpse of a huge high-ceilinged kitchen, various smaller rooms, one a study, another filled with papers and a typewriter on the desk – but he had been disinclined to linger there, and she had stored questions away for later.

He opened the door, warm air came in from the corridor as she stepped out of the conservatory, she heard him close the door behind them, then he was saying: 'Turn left at the end.' Strange how conscious you could be of someone you didn't like. He was just behind her, and so big and tall that she was extremely uneasy, her spine tingling, almost with apprehension as if he might just take it into his head to . . .

'Ah!' She jumped, startled, at the touch on her back, exactly where she had sensed – and he laughed.

'Did I frighten you? You're going the wrong way. This way. Excuse me.' He passed her, touched her elbow to redirect her, and she turned obediently. I must stop this, she thought. I'm getting as jumpy as a kitten whenever he's near. I must control it, or he'll know.

He opened a door, and she went in and looked all around her. Dismay sank her heart like a stone. What had she imagined? A library, yes, a room in a house, nicely lined with books, but this was *vast*. Rows and rows, going on for ever, stretching from floor to ceiling, hundreds and hundreds . . .

'This is it. What you expected?' He was watching her, and she saw the soft gleam of mockery in those green eyes.

Vanessa shook her head faintly. 'I thought – it's a bit larger than I imagined,' she admitted.

A crooked smile touched his mouth. 'It is rather big,' he agreed. 'Still, you look very efficient to me. You'll need old clothes. I'll bet some books are covered in dust in the far reaches.' There was a certain relish in his tone, and she looked at him. She had made up her mind, but he was rapidly undermining her resolve to be polite, cool – imperturbable. He knew all right, that was what made it worse. She swallowed hard.

'I'll begin tomorrow,' she said. 'A bit of dirt doesn't bother *me*, I assure you.' And she looked him casually up and down, and managed to smile. Because the thought of *him* getting stuck into a pile of dusty old books was funny. He had a certain fastidious air about him. If she could have managed it, she would have even laughed. But she didn't dare.

'Good.' One eyebrow lifted gently. 'Come on, I'll take you to the cellars now, and then we'll have coffee in the lounge. We mustn't keep Mrs. Banks waiting too long.'

'The cellars?' Did he think she wanted to see the wine? Or the coal? A laugh threatened to escape.

'You'll be interested, I assure you. Come on, this way.'

The stairs leading down to the cellars were at the end of a passage leading from behind the stairs. Vanessa had the thoroughly confused feeling of being utterly lost. And all the time, as Cal showed her round, she was realizing that this had been her father's home, where he had lived, had played ...

'I'll go first. The steps are rather steep. Can you see?'

'Yes, thank you.' The walls were painted white, the stairs of stone, but carpeted, so that the hollow echo of their footsteps was slightly muffled. Strip lighting threw few shadows as she followed the broad back in front of her, and reached a corridor with several doors off, all closed.

The thought that he had decided to imprison her made her look quickly round. Absurd, of course, but this man was so unpredictable that even the absurd seemed almost feasible, with him.

'This way. This is what I wanted to show you'. He opened the brown wooden door to the left, and softly, hesitantly, Vanessa walked to it, and through it, then seeing the room, gasped. For at the instant of her going in, he reached out and switched on the light, and what she saw was so unexpected, so completely *unreal*, that she could not help the exclamation.

She was standing in a gymnasium, a beautifully equipped large room with wall bars, ropes, climbing ladders, vaulting horse, all neatly shining. Large thick mats were on the floor, in the far corner was an exercise bike, in another weights and barbells, and a huge weighing machine.

Vanessa turned to him, all enmity forgotten for a moment in her complete surprise. 'It's marvellous!' she said.

'Isn't it? Mr. Maclean is a keep-fit fanatic. Comes down two or three times a week.' He walked forward and touched one of the mats with his foot, thoughtfully. 'And this is a judo mat. He's quite good at that too.'

She looked at him. 'You – are *you* his instructor?'

He shook his head. 'No, I didn't teach him. But we practise. He's good for his age.'

Vanessa knew how old her grandfather was, knew from her father. He was sixty-six. But she wasn't supposed to know, and this was the sort of thing that could give her away if she was not constantly on her guard.

'I thought Mr. Maclean would be too old—' she gestured at the mat, and was not a little dismayed to see the shrewd look Cal gave her as he answered:

'He's mid-sixties, I think. Not too old at all.' Why was he looking at her like that? She began to feel uneasy. Was this how a criminal felt, always with the disturbing idea that discovery was imminent?

'Oh, I see.' She answered him calmly, because of course he could not guess, could he? But quickly then, to cover up, in case, she added:

'So this is why you offered to teach me – because this was here?' And she regretted it immediately, because she had been trying to forget *that* idea.

'Ah, you remembered. That's right. Want your first lesson now?'

That was quite enough! Vanessa tilted her chin, and smiled – or tried to, which wasn't quite the same thing.

'Heavens, I don't think so,' she answered. 'I wouldn't dream—'

'Scared?' he said, quite softly. It was funny how clearly his words sounded when he said them like that.

She shrugged. 'I've seen you in action, remember? That was quite enough. Your enthusiasm might carry you away. I mean, I'd hate you to feel guilty if you *accidentally*—' and the emphasis on that word was intentional '—broke my arm.'

He gave her a soft, deadly smile. 'I'd be most careful, I assure you.'

'Yes, I'm sure you would. But no, thanks.' And she half turned away, with the intention of going to look at the exercise bicycle. Cal put his hand on her arm, and stopped her, quite simply.

She looked down at those fingers and said: 'Take your hand off me.'

'Make me!'

She looked at him, puzzled, and he smiled. 'Look, if I'd had lecherous intentions you wouldn't stand a chance. Learn some basic self-defence, and there'd be an element of surprise – enough for you to get away from me.'

Vanessa went very still. 'Why,' she said after a moment, 'are you so keen to teach me?'

'Because you had a damn big scare on your way here. You had no idea how to cope – and let's say I don't like to see a woman unable to look after herself. It's simply that.' And he took his hand away so that she was free to walk off, but she didn't move. Something in his words had the ring of truth. In spite of the mutual dislike, perhaps he did mean them.

'I can manage,' she said after a moment. 'If – if you went for me now, I'd just lift my knee and kick you hard—'

'And land flat on your back before you'd even connected,' he finished for her. Then, as she hesitated, disbelieving: 'Want to prove it? Go on, try it.'

She froze. 'I – wouldn't want to – I might hurt you,' she said lamely.

He laughed. 'I'll chance it. Go on.'

She shook her head. She knew that he spoke the truth. 'No. I believe you.' She looked behind her to the mat. He would have thrown her on *that*. The thought was quite sobering.

He must have read her thoughts. 'I wouldn't have thrown you hard. You'd barely have noticed. And that's another thing. You should learn how to fall – how to relax.'

'I'll think about it,' and she walked determinedly away from him. The whole thing was ridiculous! As if she would let *him* teach her how to look after herself, allow him to touch her ... But strangely, unbidden, a small excitement spread within her at the idea.

She dismissed it firmly as she stood admiring the glossy blue enamelled bicycle with its mileometer and speedometer at the side. You could tell how many 'miles' you had done, as well as at what speed. And how nice, after a day with dusty books, to come down and cycle a few miles! She smiled at the thought, and Cal Grayne was watching her, and she drew in her breath sharply.

'Have you anything else to show me?' she asked quickly. He made her feel uncomfortable when he looked like that.

'Shower in there, changing rooms next to them, that's all.'

'I see. Shall we go and have our coffee? I'm really very tired after travelling. I'd like an early night if possible.'

'I'm sure you would. Driving is tiring, isn't it?' he agreed smoothly, and they walked across the floor together. But the tension was there, and it could quite easily build up if she wasn't careful, for it was mutual, and therefore more intense, and potentially dangerous. And she wondered why it should be so, when they had first met only hours previously, but it existed, it was real – and he knew it too.

She would see things differently in the morning, Vanessa decided as she prepared for bed later that evening. She was tired – she had not been lying when she had told Cal Grayne that. A certain kind of reaction had set in after her unfortunate first meeting with him. She had a lot to be thankful to him for, but he made gratitude very difficult. She punched her pillow into shape and slid into bed, after first making sure her door was locked. The coffee had been waiting for them in the hearth of the lounge when they had returned from the gymnasium, and there had been no sign of Mrs. Banks, and for all Vanessa knew, she and her husband might not even sleep in the house. So . . . But Vanessa smiled to herself as she pulled the sheets up over her. Cal Grayne didn't even *like* her, he certainly wasn't going to try and sneak into her room. She lay on her back and looked up at the ceiling. There was a faint crack, like a thread of black cotton, running along, in a wavery line. She looked at it, trying to see any pictures in it, but it began to waver after a few minutes, and blur, and she reached up and pulled the cord that switched off the light. Just in time . . .

Waking early, Vanessa at first wondered where she was, then realization and memory flooded back, and she looked around her at the shadowy room. Strange how everything looked in the half light of the approaching dawn. Contours were soft and shadowed, and the room seemed larger, greyer. She slid out of bed and padded barefoot over the thick carpet to the window.

Outside a mist lay heavily on the ground, the rhododendrons and near trees seeming to be suspended in a sea of white. Nothing moved. She wondered where the rabbits slept. There would be more, she guessed, perhaps hundreds, for even the little of the gardens she had seen had been vast. She let the curtain fall back into place and went back to bed, there to lie awake for a while. Gradually the room lightened, the greyness gave way to softer warmer light, and she knew she would not sleep again. There was too much on her mind.

It was nearly six-thirty. Cal had told her that breakfast would be at eight-thirty. Time for bathing, dressing – and going for a walk.

There would be no harm, she decided, as she ran hot water into the shiny grey-blue bath, in just walking down the drive to the gate and back. It would give her an appetite for breakfast, and set her up for a day's work in that undoubtedly dusty library. At that thought she looked at the bath water. Was she being a little premature, having one now? Maybe evening would be better. She shrugged. She could always have another. Cal had told her, in a comparatively pleasant conversation the previous evening while they had been drinking coffee, that hot water was limitless, owing to a mountain spring which not only provided for all their needs, but also ran the dynamo that supplied the estate with electricity.

As she stepped into the bath Vanessa thought over that almost pleasant half hour spent with him. After all that had happened, it had been an oasis of truce in their invisible battle. He had set out – perhaps deliberately, she could not be sure – to be quite charming, and she had seen another, unexpected side to him.

Not certain how the day would turn out, she dressed in warm dark blue sweater and trews after her bath, and mindful of the possibilities of a chill so soon after her immersion in hot water, donned her warm furry red jacket before creeping quietly out of her room and to the stairs.

It was ghostly. Only the ticks of the grandfather clock in the hall floated up, otherwise the house appeared to be asleep. Seven-ten on a Thursday morning in June, and later today, in this house, Vanessa would meet her grandfather for the first time. And she would look at him, and talk to him, as though he were a stranger, and he would never know, until the day she left – and then it would be too late.

Her palm on the banister rail was suddenly clammy with moisture. Vanessa lifted her hand away and went on quickly down. The front door opened quietly, and cool damp air swirled in to meet her as she stood on the step for a moment. The mist had dispersed slightly. The ground, especially the gravel drive, was now visible, although thick swirls of cotton-wool mist eddied and moved near to the trees. And small dark shapes that could have been stones, but weren't, lolloped away at her approach. She smiled to herself, beautiful face softening at the sight of the baby rabbits scuttering away terrified. If only they could know that she meant them no harm!

Gravel crunched underfoot, and the early air held a promise of warmth, and Vanessa felt a tingle of excitement stir within her. She was here now, committed to her action; for better or for worse, there was no backing out.

Would she regret leaving her job as she had? Time would tell. She had been ready to leave anyway, because her boss was being uncomfortably familiar, and Vanessa had reached the stage of dreading going into his office for dictation. She closed her eyes for a moment. In a way, Cal Grayne was more right about self-defence than he knew. Men had found her utterly fascinating ever since, at the age of sixteen, her childish prettiness had fined down and changed into a stunning kind of beauty that had caused her, in a way, a lot of actual distress. Of course it was nice to know that you had this power over members of the opposite sex; Vanessa was feminine enough to enjoy that. But there was another side to

41

beauty – one her plainer friends failed to appreciate. It caused unhappiness, jealousy and suspicion on the part of her many admirers – and too among her own friends, girls who automatically avoided foursome dates, who tried to keep their boy-friends out of Vanessa's way at all costs.

And now, for the first time, she had met a man who not only seemed immune to her, but was aggressive with it. No man had ever behaved to her the way Cal Grayne did. It was not only annoying, it was intriguing. And more. Something else besides. No man had ever dared treat her like he had. Especially on the landing the previous evening, on her arrival. He had threatened her, actually *threatened* her. So used was she to complete adoration that his arrogant sureness had been even more of a jolt to her. How utterly horrible he had been! Lost in her thoughts, Vanessa was brought to an abrupt halt by the menacing growl of a dog, and looked up to see a large Alsatian standing looking at her from the side of the drive, the fur raised in a ridge along its back.

She froze. Instinct told her to stand perfectly still – and then she heard a man's voice from somewhere in the trees to her left. 'All right, Sheba. Stay!'

Relief flooded through her, and her knees went weak with reaction as she saw the tall dark-clothed figure step out from the shadowy misty trees.

He was young, broadly built and darkly handsome in a gipsy way. His glance met Vanessa's and he smiled slowly, eyes narrowing very slightly, but his tone was polite enough as he said: 'Good morning.' His accent the gentle one of the Highlander, full of grave courtesy and a certain shyness belied only by his expression – an all too familiar one to her – in his eyes.

'Good morning. Is this your dog?'

'Aye,' he nodded towards it. 'Away home now, Sheba.' The Alsatian looked at him, then padded, reluctantly it seemed, away. She let out her breath in a deep sigh.

'I was a little – nervous,' she admitted.

'Yes. But you see, Sheba didn't expect to see anyone. This is private property, I'm afraid.' He said it politely, not as if accusing her of trespassing, but merely pointing out a fact.

'Yes, I know. I'm staying here.'

Dark eyes met hers in sudden startling challenge. 'Then you – are you the lady who's come to do the books?'

'Yes.' And his laugh startled her so that she stared hard at him.

'I'm sorry.' He sobered suddenly as if realizing. 'I am laughing, you see, because I was asked if I would find a little time to help the new lady, but I tried to get out of it.' He smiled slowly, charmingly. 'But now,' and he shrugged, 'I can see I was mistaken.'

There was something about him that was attractive, in a rugged way – and something else, all too familiar, but Vanessa dimissed that firmly. It was so nice to meet a man who wasn't intent on being as rude as possible.

'I'm sorry,' she said, puzzled. 'Help me? I'm afraid I don't see—'

'With the books. Lifting them down,' he explained patiently. 'There are so many on high shelves, and difficult for a woman to manage.'

Light dawned. She nodded. 'Oh, I see. I hadn't thought of that.'

'So when do you start?'

'Today. But don't you have a job?'

'Och, yes. I am gardener here, with my father and uncle. But they will manage without me.' He moved forward towards her. He wasn't quite as tall as Cal Grayne, but he was broader and stronger-looking. He stopped in front of Vanessa, not too close, and went on: 'I am Laurie Mackenzie.' He was waiting to hear her name, that was obvious, but he wasn't going to ask. Not like *that man* Cal, who had demanded her name. And why, she thought, should that memory come back to tease her now?

'Vanessa Collins.' She smiled, and held out her hand. His clasp was warm and firm.

'I'll away now, Miss Collins, but I'll be up to the big house later — will you be starting at nine, or thereabouts?'

'I suppose so. Mr Maclean isn't here yet. Mr. Grayne is in charge at the moment.' She didn't know why she had said it, except perhaps the urge to discover something, about the unknown man she had yet to meet.

'Ach, *him*.' The intonation was unmistakable, and for a moment she thought he referred to her grandfather, his employer, then, at his next words, knew her mistake.

'I'll come directly into the library and begin. If that one sees me, he'll quite possibly tell me to — leave.' He had been going to say something else, and thought better of it.

'Mr. Grayne? Why?'

Laurie Mackenzie laughed. 'No, I've said enough. Until we meet later, Miss Collins.' And he raised one arm in a gesture of farewell, turned, and vanished into the dark misty greenness of the trees.

Vanessa stood there for a moment before walking on. She was curious now.

She watched Cal Grayne at breakfast, tempted to mention her encounter with Laurie Mackenzie, but afraid that if she did, Cal would get out of her the fact that he was coming to the library to help her. And the prospect of lifting books from the top shelves single-handed was slightly daunting, now that she really thought about it. So, wisely, Vanessa said nothing. But the thought of why Laurie should dislike Cal was intriguing. Was it mutual? That was another question – and she didn't realize, just how soon it would be answered, or in what way.

CHAPTER THREE

THE library was quiet and empty when Vanessa went in with Cal at just after nine o'clock. The sun slanted in through the tall french windows, and at the side, the huge bay, making paths of gold across the red carpet, but not touching the furthest recesses of books. She looked around her, fighting dismay. A daunting task indeed, but one she had undertaken to do, in spite of all other factors. There was a long table in the centre of the room, covered with green baize. On it lay an overall. Cal picked it up and handed it to her.

'Mrs. Banks looked this out for you,' he said. 'It will help protect your clothes.' His tone was cool, quite impersonal, yet once again, as always, Vanessa was aware of a disturbing element in the very air around them, an indefinable tension she neither liked nor understood.

'Thanks.' It was a pink nylon flowered coat-type overall, barely reaching her hips, but it would help. She looked at the table. 'I'll put the books on there, will I?'

'Yes. Paper, cards, everything you need are over there.' He strode over to a sideboard and put his hand on boxes of stationery. Then he asked: 'You'll need help when it comes to the upper shelves, won't you?'

She had not been going to mention it, but now it would have been foolish not to. 'Someone is coming to help me,' she answered – and watched his face.

He frowned. 'What do you mean?'

'I went for a walk before breakfast and met a man

called Laurie Mackenzie. He said he'd been asked to help—' She wasn't allowed to finish. It was really a surprise to her that Cal had allowed her to get that far.

'Him!' It was said in exactly the same way as Laurie's exclamation.

Vanessa widened her eyes innocently. 'Is there something wrong?'

Cal Grayne looked at her. There was no expression on his face at all, but she sensed a dark anger, well controlled. 'No,' he answered. 'Only I'd watch it if I were you. You could have trouble.'

'Trouble? What sort of trouble?' She was intrigued – as well as getting a small, feminine satisfaction out of being able to act just a shade stupid.

But she had forgotten just what this man could be like.

'Oh, come off it,' he said bluntly. 'Don't give me the wide-eyed innocent expression. It doesn't wash with me. You know damn well what I mean – or should do. You're old enough. Or did you think those two motorcyclists wanted you to pick heather with them?'

Vanessa fought for calm. 'You're *disgusting*!' she breathed, voice low, because if she spoke any louder he would notice the tremor in her voice.

'If it shakes some sense into you – yes, I am. I won't always be around to rescue you, you know. Laurie Mackenzie is a wolf, that's all. I hope you can cope with passes.'

'Oh, I can. I've had enough experience with dealing with them, thanks!' Her confidence was returning. Her beautiful dark eyes flashed fire. 'You'll be telling me next not to encourage him. You implied *that* yesterday too.'

'All right. Don't encourage him. I've enough to do without listening for you yelling for help.'

'Why don't you go, and leave me alone?' she demanded angrily, fists clenching at her sides. Oh, the sheer arrogance of the man!

'Save your punches for him.' He was watching her hands, and a slight cynical smile touched his wide mouth. 'I've told you what will happen if you start on me.'

'Go *away*!'

'I'm going. Lunch is at one. Coffee at eleven. Mrs. Banks will bring it in.' He went to the door, opened it, and then was gone. The door closed silently. Vanessa stared at it, feelings mixed. She had never met anyone quite like Cal Grayne before. He frightened her.

She turned after a few moments and walked across to the library shelves, looking up at the rows and rows in front of her. Some of the books looked terribly old and fragile, the leather bindings faded and worn. She lifted one book down and opened it, after first blowing the light film of dust from the top. It was a bound magazine for the year 1767 – she had to mentally translate from the Roman figures on the title page. The paper was yellowy brown, freckled with age, the print small but very clear. Vanessa held the book with care, and as always, with anything so very old, a sense of history communicated itself to her. It was tempting her to sit down and read, but she knew she must not. Perhaps at eleven, when coffee came, then she would.

She was about to put the overall on when there came a loud rap at the door, and Laurie Mackenzie walked in. For just a second, with Cal's words coming vividly to mind, she felt shocked, then she smiled. Absurd to let that man make her nervous!

'Hello,' she greeted him. 'I was just about to begin.'

'Hello,' he smiled. It was a shy, nice smile, not at all wolfish.

'I've been looking around at the shelves,' she said. 'I'll be glad of your help, I think.'

'I know.' He was just watching her, and although she was used to it, she nevertheless felt a slight tingle of apprehension. He wouldn't, would he? Make a pass at her? She knew it was only too possible, even with the nicest, quietest-looking men. Which was why she found Cal Grayne's behaviour towards her so baffling. He didn't look as if he would ever even think of getting fresh with her – and yet he seemed normal enough – male enough. Very much so, in fact, she thought, almost wryly.

But this man Laurie was different again. He was here to help her, and it would only complicate matters if she had to watch him all the time. Vanessa resolved to quash anything – even the slightest remark that was capable of misinterpretation – at the outset, so that he would not be in any doubt.

She gave him a bright, very impersonal smile. 'I'm thinking of beginning at this end—' she pointed, '—and I'd best stack them on the table, then go through them.'

'I'll get them down for you.' He wore a tartan lumber jacket which he took off to reveal a dark blue sweater. His chest was broad, arms strong-looking. He put the jacket over a chair, walked along to the ladder that was fixed on runners further down the room, and brought it back.

The next quarter of an hour was busily spent removing books from the top shelves, down to the table. He worked quietly and efficiently, handling the books with care, stacking them neatly, and when there were nearly a hundred lying on the baize-covered surface, he stopped and looked at Vanessa.

'That'll be enough, I think,' he said. 'You need room to write, don't you?'

'Yes. Thanks.'

'I'll help you.' Vanessa looked at him. How did he mean? He saw the look and grinned.

'I'll help you get them in order, ready to list. That's what you're going to do first, isn't it?'

'Well, yes, but—'

'Then it'll be quicker with the two of us.'

She shook her head, bemused. 'Fine. Thank you. I just didn't imagine—'

'No? I can read, you know.'

'I didn't mean *that*!' she protested quickly, then she saw his smile, and knew he was joking.

'I know you didn't. It'll be a change for me. And old books are fascinating.'

'Then we'd better get started. Actually you might have better ideas than me. I was going to list all the titles and authors or other reference, if any, then put the books back in order with reference slips every ten or so—'

'Yes. But I've got a better idea. Suppose we—' and he went on, calmly and concisely outlining a plan, touching the books as he spoke, lifting one and opening it, looking at it, touching the paper, and Vanessa thought, watching him: He's nice. I wonder why he and Cal don't get on? Perhaps just a natural antagonism. It often happens

– it has already with Cal and me, this prickly dislike that makes me uneasy.

And then there was not much time for talking or thinking as they set to work. So engrossed were they both that it was almost a shock when Mrs. Banks brought in coffee at eleven. Seeing Laurie, she gave a big sniff, said: 'I suppose I'd better get you some as well,' and vanished.

He grinned at Vanessa who was eyeing her coffee thirstily, wondering if he would think it bad manners if she just took a sip now . . .

'You'd not believe she likes me, would you?' he said.

Cal had made an observation about her bark being worse than her bite. Perhaps it was. 'No,' Vanessa shook her head gently. 'Does she?'

'Aye, in her own way. You should see her husband. Never says a word if he can help it. Still, she's a damn good cook. That's why the old man wouldn't let her go.'

This was an opportunity, and Vanessa took it. 'I've never met Mr. Maclean,' she said. 'Is he all right to work for?'

'Oh yes, he's fine – when you get to know him.' But there was that something in his words that prompted Vanessa.

'What exactly do you mean?'

'Well, he's a bit fierce at first. He'll maybe not be with you, you being a girl, but he can be with men.'

Her heart sank. What had she let herself in for? Then came a further thought – but what had she expected? Certainly not a gentle old man. Not after what her father had said . . .

'What does he look like?'

Laurie frowned thoughtfully. 'Quite tall, lean but wiry, if you know what I mean. Mind you, he keeps very fit. Walks miles – and you'll maybe have seen the gym?'

'Yes, I have. Cal Grayne showed me last night.' Some imp of mischief prompted her to add, she would never know why: 'He says he'll teach me some judo.'

Laurie's face darkened. He was about to say something when the door opened again, and Mrs. Banks came in with a second cup of coffee.

'Here y'are.' She set it down on the table, gave Vanessa a hard stare, said: 'Lunch at one, y'know,' and went out.

Vanessa wondered what Laurie had been going to say, for in the few moments that Mrs. Banks had been in the room, he had made an apparent effort to calm himself. She had been sure he'd been about to explode before. Now he said, almost normally: 'Aye, well, I'd not be letting him bother if I were you.'

'Really? Why not?'

He looked at her hard. 'Because he's a wolf, that's why. It's just an excuse—' and he stopped, very suddenly, and picked up his coffee cup.

Vanessa would never know how she kept her face straight. First Cal's warning about this man, now Laurie warning her about Cal! It could be almost funny, if only they weren't so deadly serious about it – but perhaps even that had its humorous side.

'Oh dear, is he?' She watched him bring out cigarettes, and shook her head when he offered her one. 'No, thanks.'

'Do you mind if I do?'

'Not at all. Why do you say he's a wolf? He hasn't seemed so to me.'

Laurie looked up at her. 'Because he's bloody clever with it,' and there was some quality of anger now in his face. 'But you'd better ask my sister about *that*. I wouldn't know.'

'Your sister?' She could only repeat the words, for her mouth was dry.

'Aye. She's left now, gone to Aberdeen – but she could tell you a few things about Cal Grayne.'

'How long ago – I mean when did she leave?'

'A month or so past. She's away working at my aunt's hotel. Says she won't come back as long as *he's* here.' He looked at the door as if hoping the subject of his thoughts would come through. Vanessa felt most odd, so she took a good drink of coffee to soothe her. She was torn between the desire to know more – and the strange urge to tell Laurie she didn't want to hear another word. But he resolved the problem for her by standing up and stubbing his half-smoked cigarette out into an ashtray on the sideboard, then drinking his coffee in one long swallow.

'Aye, well, I've said enough,' he remarked. 'It's back to work for me. I have to go out after lunch, so I'll make sure you have all the books down that you'll need for today.'

'Of course. Thank you. Do you know what time Mr. Maclean is returning?'

He shrugged. 'No idea. Mrs. Banks would tell you, though. Why do you ask?'

'Well, he is my employer. I – I just wondered.'

'You make the most of the time before he comes.' He gave her a dry smile. 'Och no, I'm only joking. He's no'

53

so bad at all. Just—' He paused, then shrugged. 'Well, it's difficult to put into words, but he seems sometimes as though he's looking through you, as if you're not really there, or as if he's miles away – and it's most odd.'

Vanessa listened in silence. And where did he go when he was far away? Was he perhaps regretting the past, and what had gone? Things which could now never be altered? Perhaps she would never know. Something stirred inside her. She wanted to meet this man, this grandfather of hers – and yet at the same time, she wanted to run away, and forget that she had ever come to Deanston House. She looked down at her hands. No, that was something she must never do. She would stick it out now. She *would*.

'Eh, you're all right?'

'What? Oh, I'm sorry. Yes.' Vanessa shook her head, and gave Laurie a smile, forgetting her resolve to keep cool with him. 'I was just thinking.' She saw his face change, saw warm awareness flicker in those dark eyes, and she looked quickly away and picked up a book.

Then, minutes later, it happened. She had gone to a lower shelf to check on a book that had been replaced. Straightening up, she was aware of him standing right behind her even before she turned, and she took a deep breath. Then she felt his hand on her arm and she moved slightly, and began: 'Yes, what—' but the words were halted as he bent his face and kissed her, putting his hands on her shoulders as he did so.

Vanessa pushed him away, not particularly angry. 'Why did you do that?'

'An impulse.' Laurie grinned, and looked down at her, and his face was shadowed.

'Please don't do it again,' she breathed. 'We're supposed to be working together, remember? And that's all.'

'I'll try and remember. Would it be more welcome to you if it was *him*?' And he gave a contemptuous jerk of his head which left Vanessa in no doubt as to who he meant.

She suppressed a quick irrational flare of anger at his words. 'Certainly *not*! And it's none of your business anyway.'

'That's good. I'd not like to think of him kissing you.'

'Then why don't you think about your work instead?' she answered coolly.

A quick smile crossed his face. 'You've got spirit, haven't you? I like a girl with a bit of fire in her.'

Vanessa moved away from him, towards the table. She put a book down then turned towards him.

'Listen,' she said. 'You're getting too personal for my liking. Now, I appreciate your help with the books – but I'll make darn sure I manage without your assistance if I'm going to have to be watching you all the time. Am I making myself clear?' Her dark eyes sparkled, her cheeks were pink, and she stood very tall and straight, a slender figure of young womanhood, as she faced the approaching Laurie.

It was at that moment that Cal walked in. There was an electric, throbbing silence for several seconds. Vanessa thought wildly: It must be obvious! Then he spoke, his dark deep voice cutting through the tense silence with the words:

'I came to see if you were managing all right.'

She turned to him. 'Yes, thanks.' But she couldn't

smile – even if she had wanted to. Cal's gaze turned to Laurie, and it was of steel.

'Any trouble with the books?'

Laurie met the stare with his own, equally hard. Vanessa, watching, thought: They're like two dogs meeting in the street, bristling silently, sizing each other up, ready to snarl and snap at any second. And there was nothing amusing in the thought, for the dislike was mutual, almost tangible.

'None at all, thanks. We're getting on fine – just fine.' The grin that accompanied the words spoke volumes, and she took a deep breath. She stood very still, instinct telling her not to speak, to wait, for what was going on was in a way nothing to do with her.

Cal's face gave nothing away. He merely nodded. 'Good. Then I'll leave you to it.' And he went out, a tall man with a well controlled temper, that was obvious even from the back of him, visible in the angle of the broad powerful shoulders. The door closed, and Laurie looked at Vanessa, and gave a low whistle.

'Good job he didn't come in a few seconds before,' he said. 'I wonder what he'd have made of me kissing you?'

'I don't know.' She looked at him, surprising herself by her sudden knowledge. 'You'd have liked that, wouldn't you? You'd have enjoyed a bit of trouble.'

'I'd like the chance to punch him one, if that's what you mean – yes,' he nodded, his jaw tight.

'Then I'd better warn you,' she looked at him, a slight frown on her forehead, '*I* had trouble on the way here – two youths on motor-bikes. He knocked them both for six – *both* of them – and one had a bottle. I'd not seen anything like it before – I hope I don't again. You may dislike him, but he's not soft. He's a lot tougher than you imagine.'

'I can deal with him,' Laurie said softly. 'Just give me a fair chance, that's all.'

Vanessa watched him. He looked tough and strong. Why, oh, why were men so keen on fighting? Why did they have to reduce everything to a physical level? She shrugged, weary of the discussion, which was in a way quite disturbing to her. Perhaps, she thought, it's a reminder of what happened – and what nearly happened – yesterday. But even as she thought it, she knew it wasn't entirely that.

From then until lunch, Laurie's behaviour was perfectly correct. He moved dozens of books so that Vanessa would not need to lift any more down that day, however fast she worked, and he didn't attempt to touch her or even come too near her. At ten to one he said :'I must away now. But I'll be back in the morning – if that's all right?'

She looked at him. 'Fine, thank you. Mr. Maclean should be back by then. You're sure he doesn't mind?'

'It was his idea in the first place. He'll soon know why I changed my mind when he sees you,' he smiled softly. 'He has an eye for a pretty woman.'

But she was not in the mood for any kind of sweet talk. 'Right, I'll see you about nine, then, shall I? I must go and wash now, ready for lunch. 'She slipped off the overall and hung it over a chair before Laurie could make any move to help her. He picked up his jacket from the chair, and together they went out of the library.

The dining-room was empty when Vanessa – rather shyly – walked into it ten minutes later. The first thing she noticed was that only two places were set. Two. Her heart did a funny flip. So her grandfather had not yet returned! She went and sat down in the place she had occupied the previous evening, and a wave of sudden inexplicable loneliness swept over her. She looked up, and Cal Grayne was coming through the open doorway, and she made an effort to hide the pain in her eyes, lest he see it.

He sat down opposite her and there was an odd expression on his face, a deep searching look in his eyes, almost as if he *knew*. Then his words shattered the fragile mood. 'I'm sorry if I walked in at the wrong moment before,' he said, but he looked anything but regretful.

'Not at all,' she answered. 'We were busy doing the books, that's all.'

'Were you? It looked like a blazing row in progress – but it's none of my business.'

'You are so right,' she agreed sweetly. 'It isn't.'

Mrs. Banks came in then and effectively silenced anything that Cal might have been about to say. She left them soup and rolls, announced:

'I'll be back in a few minutes. It's cheese soufflé, so be ready for it,' and went out.

And if I were here with anyone else, thought Vanessa, we'd be laughing quietly about her now. But with him – prickly hostility. And why, oh, why was it so?

She bent to her soup, which was very hot, and as she touched the plate there came a loud shriek from outside, chill and frightening. The plate jerked, it tipped up, and hot soup gushed over Vanessa's right hand. She cried out in sudden pain, seeing the hot red liquid covering her hand – feeling it – and Cal stood up, leaned over the table, took her wrist in his own hand and tipped the contents of the water jug over it.

Then he was round by her side as she stood, gasping, holding to the table for support as everything went frighteningly round. 'Sit down.' His voice was grittily commanding. 'Put your head well down between your knees.' She heard him moving plates out of reach as she obeyed, helpless to resist. 'I'm going to get something. I'll not be a moment.'

He was gone. The waves of pain were frightening, but she stayed in her chair. There had been something in his voice she dared not disobey. He was back almost immediately with a box which he put on the table and opened. The next moment he was smearing cold yellow ointment over her hand.

'The shriek you heard was the peacock,' he said. 'I guess it's a bit of a shock the first time. You'll get used to it.'

'Peacock!' she repeated in a whisper, watching him work, biting her lip to stop the gasp of pain.

'That a bit better?' He was quite cool and impersonal, and at least the hostility had gone, for the moment anyway.

'Yes, thanks.' She looked at the table, all swimming with a mixture of soup and water, and tears filled her eyes. 'I'm sorry—'

'Forget it.' He looked at the table too. 'Mrs. Banks will clear that lot up in a moment.'

'You've not had your soup,' she said guiltily. He was folding clean white lint round her hand, and the greasy cream was already taking the edge off the pain. Then bandage, deftly applied as she watched.

'No,' he said. 'But it was too hot anyway. Do you want it? I can get some more.'

She shook her head. 'I'll have some soufflé, I think. I'm not – not very hungry now.'

'No, you wouldn't be. You want to go and lie down for a while?'

She looked sharply up at him, seeking the sarcasm. He frowned. 'What is it?'

Vanessa shook her head faintly. 'Nothing. I thought you were being—' she faltered.

'Sarcastic?' A grim smile touched the corner of his mouth. 'No, I wasn't. You've gone very white – shock. It'll pass. But it wouldn't do you any harm to put your feet up for a half hour or so. No one will mind.'

'No, thank you. I'll be better after I've eaten, honestly.' But she was beginning to shiver, and it was hard to hide the fact.

Silently he put his hands on her elbows and lifted her out of the chair with the words: 'Over here – my chair. And get my soup down you. *Now.*' There was no refusing him. She was too weak.

The soup was still hot, but not too much, and it warmed and filled her immediately. Mrs. Banks brought in the soufflé, took one look at the mess on the table and told them to move along a bit while she sorted it out, an order which both obeyed, because it was sensible.

Vanessa's hand throbbed and hurt quite a lot, but she thought she was managing to conceal it from the man who ate quietly opposite her, and who didn't show any signs of his usual aggression.

After they had finished he said, going round to Vanessa's side of the table: 'Come on, we'll have coffee in the lounge. All right?'

'Yes.' But she swayed slightly as she reached the door, and heard his small exasperated exclamation from behind her. She felt a warm hand on her arm.

'Why are you so *stubborn*?' he whispered.

'I don't know what you mean,' but she did. The walls at either side of them swayed alarmingly as they made their way to the hall, and across to the lounge, and she was almost glad of that strong hand on her arm ... almost ...

'I'm all right, really.' She sat down as she said it, and looked up at him. But she could not hide the tears of pain in her eyes. Without a word he turned and went out of the room, leaving her alone.

I've frightened him away, she thought. Good!

But he was back a minute later with two cups of coffee. 'I'm taking you to the doctor's in the village,' he told her as he put her cup down beside her on a small table. 'So drink up. Then we'll go.'

'But I don't—'

'Please don't argue,' he said, quite gently for him. 'Because we're going even if I have to carry you out to the damned car.'

She looked down at the full cup and picked it up slowly. There was no doubt that he meant what he said. She knew he would do it, and almost smiled at the thought of being *carried* out – by *him*!

'All right.' She took a swallow and blinked because it was so hot.

'Cigarette?'

'I don't smoke – not often anyway, thanks.'

She heard the lighter click, the sweet aromatic smell of new tobacco, and she didn't look up, because she couldn't. For some reason her heart was beating faster than usual, and she felt as if he would hear the beats if she looked up at him.

Her face was warm, and she wondered, quite absurdly, if she had a temperature. But you didn't with shock, did you? She put her hand to her forehead, and it was burning.

'Are you all right?' His voice seeemed to be coming from a great distance away, as if she was going deaf, and she looked quickly up, to see him reaching out to take the nearly full cup from her.

'Yes – yes – it's just—' she swallowed hard. Heavens, what was happening to her? The room seemed to be swimming in grey mist, and she put her hand up in a desperate effort to hold on to something – anything – then was caught and held as she heard Cal's voice coming from a great way away ... But she never heard what he said.

She woke to find herself lying down on the long brocade-covered settee, and she opened her eyes slowly. Cal was standing looking down at her, face expressionless. Their eyes met. 'You're all right,' he said. 'You fainted, that's all. Nothing to worry about.'

'I've never fainted in my life,' Vanessa said.

He gave her a crooked smile. 'You have now. Don't worry. Stay there for a few minutes, then we'll go.'

She didn't want to go in the car with him. She knew that – but she didn't understand why. And she couldn't say either, because he had threatened to take her out by force if necessary. Strength was gradually returning, her head becoming clearer. After a few minutes she looked up at him. 'I'm all right now,' she said.

'Then we'll go. The sooner you get that scald treated,

the better.'

He fetched her coat for her, and drove the car round to the front of the house while she waited in the lounge. She heard the tyres scrunch to a halt on the gravel and went to the door, walking carefully, because the floor still had a slight tendency to rise and fall with every step she took.

Minutes later they were travelling down the drive, not fast, but not slowly either.

'How far is the village?' she asked after a few minutes, as they neared the gateway.

'About eight miles. We'll soon be there. Is the pain very bad?'

She pulled a little face. 'Not too much. I don't know why I passed out. I've never done so before.'

'Perhaps you've never been hurt as much before. It's a natural defence mechanism of the brain's.'

'Have you ever fainted?'

He looked at her briefly, as if considering the question. Then he gave her a slight smile. 'Once, yes – but I don't intend to tell you about it. Not just now anyway,' and he looked at her hand as he said it.

It was odd. Some of the tension seemed to have gone and yet there was something disquieting about the atmosphere in the car. Vanessa moved uneasily, aware that this was the man she didn't like, that she was being forced to travel in his car with him – something she had imagined she would never do. And she found herself waiting – but she knew not for what.

Then minutes later she found out. He said very casually, as he drove down the narrow road towards the main one: 'He'll be back first thing in the morning, not today.'

She knew who he referred to. She knew that straight away. But she asked, as if mildly surprised: 'Who? Mr. Maclean?'

'Who else?' He gave her a swift sidelong glance. 'Your employer. I thought you'd be wondering about him.'

'Yes, I was.' Her heart was beating faster than usual. There was *something* in his words. She couldn't put her finger on it, but it was there. And the pain in her hand was having the effect of dulling her wits slightly, so that she had to think well before she spoke. 'You – you said he'd be back today.'

'He would have been, but he was delayed. Er – you've not met him yet, you say?'

What was he getting at? Vanessa looked out of the window on her left, seeing the trees flash past in a green blur that barely registered. She didn't realize she was clenching the wrist of her scalded hand until she touched the palm by mistake. Then she looked down.

'No, of course not. How – how could I? I come from London.'

'I know you do. And your name is Vanessa Collins.' And he smiled. She felt herself freeze. He had paused ever so slightly before Collins, and it had not been accidental. It had been done quite deliberately.

She took a deep breath, a kind of fear touching her momentarily. He couldn't guess – could he? No, the idea was absurd. But she wished now she hadn't come. Her presentiment had been right. It was almost uncanny. The hand began to throb again, and she felt wretched. If only it didn't hurt so much, she would be able to cope with any insinuations made by this very disturbing man; as it was, it was almost too much effort to try and think of good sound answers.

But she tried. 'Yes. And yours is Cal Grayne. Very unusual,' she forced a smile. 'Spelt GRAYNE?'

'Yes. Callum Grayne. My father was a Scot, my mother Rumanian.'

Despite the other matter, Vanessa was intrigued. And it kept him off the subject . . .

'You mean you're half Rumanian?'

'Yes.' She looked at him. She should have known he had foreign blood in him. It was there in the arrogant tilt of his chin, the darkness, and those unusual eyes. Deep fascinating green, looking straight at her, reading her mind . . .

'No—' and she didn't know she had said it aloud until he said:

'No what?'

'Nothing. Nothing.' She looked away out of the window.

'And your parents? Where are they from?' It could have been just a polite social question, but she was jumpy enough to suspect everything he said or did now.

She took a deep breath. 'My mother—' her story had gone right out of her head. The complete life history she had made up for just this eventuality. Her mind was a complete blank. She put her hand to her forehead. She had just one slight weapon. 'I'm s-sorry,' she stumbled, 'my hand – it's so p-painful again.' And it was true, only partly, but at least it would give her time to *think*. Not even *he* would keep on at her now – would he?

And if he didn't believe her, he managed to hide it well. He increased speed immediately. 'We'll be there in a minute,' he said. She sat back and tried to relax. She knew this was only a temporary respite. How long would it last?

The doctor was a man of few words, but kind, and when Vanessa walked out of his surgery, her hand was much less painful. He had shaken a few white pills into a carton, written a prescription for ointment, and told her to rest the hand for a few days.

Cal was waiting in the hallway of the rather dark forbidding house, sitting on one of the row of straight wooden chairs that lined the hall. He stood up when Vanessa went towards him. 'Better now?' he asked, eyes appraising her levelly.

'Yes, thank you. He said you did the right thing pouring cold water on – there'll be very few blisters. I've got to rest it for a couple of days, and it should be fine.'

'We'll have to find you another job instead of cataloguing then,' it was said half jokingly as he opened the door for her. She looked at him.

'You won't. I'm left-handed – I can still write. I've got a prescription here. Is there a chemist's shop?'

'Down at the other end of the village. I'll get the car.'

'Can't we walk?'

'Do you feel strong enough?' Vanessa looked quickly at him. Was there the faintest tinge of irony – or was it her guilty imagination working overtime again?

'It'll do me good, I imagine. It's a lovely day.' And that was quite true. The sun shone from a cloudless sky, glittering on the dark waters of the loch beside them to their left. To their right the endless row of cottages with tiny gardens. Cal had left the car in a garage forecourt next door to the doctor's. He was obviously well known, for the proprietor, seeing them arrive, had come out from the office to greet him and inquire did he need petrol or oil.

'Fine, let's go.'

The pavement was non-existent most of the time, but the road surface was good, and while several cars passed them, it was not really busy. Vanessa looked away over to her left, trying not to be too aware of the tall dark stranger by her side. The hills at the far edge of the water stretched away into hazy distance. The outlines were stark and clear nearer to, and the beauty of it all caught her breath in her throat. To live here, and to be able to look out over this every day!

'It *is* pretty powerful, isn't it?'

She looked at him, startled. 'What is?'

'The view. All of it. The effect it has on you for the first time.'

'Yes, it's terrific.' But inside she felt dismay. Why did he have to be so astute? It was almost uncanny the way he seemed to read what she was thinking. Oh, why did he have to be here – now – at Deanston House? But there was no way to get an answer. She would have to be careful, very careful, she knew that. To give her time to collect her scattered wits, she said something she had been intending to say for quite a few minutes.

'Thank you very much for bringing me here. I realize it was the sensible thing to do now.'

'It's quite all right. No trouble.' He smiled quite charmingly at her, and her heart did a funny skip and jump. Now why should I have this reaction? she thought wildly. He's really an *awful* man – and yet just then, when he smiled, it was so different. He really can be attractive if he wants to. Which made all the more puzzling what happened later. But Vanessa could not foresee that.

Cal waited until they were half-way up the road to the house, at roughly the spot where he had signalled her to halt the previous day, and stopped the car. She looked at him, startled.

'I thought you'd like to see the view from here. That's quite something too.' Immediately she suspected his motives, remembering the subtle questions before, that she had only stopped by pretending her hand hurt. But there was nothing she could do about it. She waited numbly while he got out, and walked round to her side. The door opened and he stood there waiting. Pleasantly, none of the aggression in sight. And she was very suspicious and wary. There was only one way to play it; cool.

'Thank you.' She stepped out, and smiled at him – her best smile, the one that always gave Mr. Murton a near heart attack, the one that nearly brought a building site to a standstill because a friend had made a remark that she had found terribly amusing just as they were passing it.

Cal smiled back, and his eyes were warm and friendly. 'That's better,' he said amiably. 'It's no good fighting all the time, is it?'

'Why, no,' Vanessa agreed, 'it isn't.' She looked around. 'Where—?'

'Up here,' he pointed. 'If we walk up here we get the most magnificent view in Scotland – at least in my opinion. You can make it?' This almost anxiously, as if he really cared – and she was beginning to think that perhaps he did.

'Yes.' They set off walking upwards, to the outline of

hill against sky, springy heather underfoot, windswept trees and bushes behind them, the air fresh and tangy with wind from the sea. Vanessa took a deep breath, then, as they reached the top of the slight slope, she stood still and looked round her in appreciative wonder.

'Oh, yes,' she said. 'Oh, yes, it's beautiful, isn't it?' The rolling hills swept all around them, down to a distant sea, with a glorious backdrop of misty blue mountains, and the greens of the grass were different shaded and dramatic, and far away, craggy rocks surrounded the loch side, so that the water shushed round their base in white foam.

And Cal looked at her and smiled again, and she wondered briefly why he was making such an effort. And then he spoke. 'I know your name's not Vanessa Collins,' he remarked, almost casually. 'So what is it?'

CHAPTER FOUR

THE shock was great – at first, just for a few sickening seconds, then Vanessa recovered, and a piece of very good advice flashed into her mind: Attack is the best method of defence.

She turned swiftly to him, the fear evaporating, for she had a lot to lose – and she didn't intend to let this man spoil the plans that had taken so long to mature. A certain kind of calm came over her; instinctively she knew she possessed advantages he could not defeat. Her very femininity was one. She could use her charm to its full effect if she had to – but not yet. Now was the time for the moral indignation, the anger at this sheer impertinence. For that was how she would feel if she were completely innocent – angry.

'I *beg* your pardon!' The words came quite easily. 'Have you gone mad? Or are you just trying to be rude?'

Cal Grayne stood there, stuck his hands in his pockets, and looked at her. 'Good try,' he said. 'Righteous indignation becomes you.'

Vanessa felt her treacherous temper rising fast. She tried hard to control it. Better not to genuinely lose her temper. Pretence was one thing, but she might say something she regretted if she really went to town on him. She was breathing fast now, she knew her cheeks were pink.

Cal Grayne watched her, his face giving nothing away. Nothing showed, the strong features remained calm and slightly hard.

'You've just made a ridiculous accusation. Would you mind telling me why?'

A brief smile came and went. 'Certainly. You remember the first time we met?'

'Could I ever forget it? You are referring, of course, to the way you so *rudely* asked me my name?'

'Was I rude? Well, perhaps I was. I was pretty furious with you—'

'Are you going to give me your life story?' she managed, honey-sweet. 'Because if so—'

'No, I'm not. But you asked. You didn't even know what your name was—'

'I explained why. I don't tell strangers—'

'Oh, come on! What sort of stranger was I? I'd just got you out of a sticky situation. Why should you be frightened of me?'

'I was – very nervous. And if you ever let me finish a sentence, it'll be a miracle!' She was adjusting rapidly to this new and rather unnerving situation, dredging a kind of confidence out of fear. 'Let's say I didn't *want* you to know my real name. And that's all I'm going to say. You're a bully – the worst kind, because you pick a time to make your disgusting innuendoes when I'm not feeling at my best. That's typical! I find your remarks most offensive – and I have no intention of staying here with you. Look at the view on your own!' And with that she turned round and walked away, determinedly going back towards the car, uneasily aware that if he chose to make her walk, there would not be much she could do about it. But the main thing was to *appear* confident. Even if you trembled inside, as long as you managed to hide it, you stood a better chance of winning most battles. And this was one – a clash of personalities; his hard, ruthless, probing; hers on the defensive because of what she knew and he didn't.

He was after her immediately. He didn't wait, just came down after her with long strides, and took her left arm in a grip that was quietly steely. And he stopped her just like that so that she had to stand still. Vanessa turned. Temper flared genuinely this time, real and instant.

'Take your dirty hands off me – you *swine*!'

His eyes narrowed. 'You've got a rare old temper.'

'With you – yes! You're despicable!'

Then he did the unforgivable – he laughed. Vanessa wrenched her arm free with all her strength. 'You're hateful,' she gasped. 'Hateful! Leave me alone—' and then, to her own utter horror, she burst into tears. Blinded by them, she ran the last few yards to the car and pulled the door open. Everything was swimming, unreal, as if in a dream, and she waited almost disinterestedly for Cal to come and yank her out. She didn't care any more. He was quite simply a brute.

His door slammed, she felt rather than saw him beside her, the clean tweedy scent of his jacket was almost attractive. Then—

'All right, you made your point. For God's sake stop crying!'

Surprised, she stopped in mid-sob, gave a little gulp, and blinked hard. 'You – you made me,' she managed, after a few moments. She began to fumble in her bag for her handkerchief, but it was difficult, for her hand was very clumsy.

'Here.' One was thrust at her, and she put it to her face to dab the tears away. Oh, how I hate him, she thought, and had to stop herself from saying it out loud.

There came a click, and the next moment the car was flooded with sound as pop music blared out. Cal turned the volume down and looked at Vanessa, who managed to glare back at him, tears still glistening in her eyes.

'All right, little wildcat. Calmed down now?' he inquired softly.

She wondered, almost abstractedly, what he would do now if she hit him hard. The temptation was so great that she had to hold tight to her bag to stop herself from doing it. Perhaps he didn't really expect an answer, for he switched on the engine and the powerful motor throbbed with life. He touched the handbrake and they moved forward with increasing speed along the road back to Deanston House. Vanessa sat very still, leaning back against the seat, handkerchief tight in hand. She felt utterly exhausted. And her grandfather was coming home in the morning.

Later that evening as she lay on her bed before getting ready for dinner, Vanessa found the events of the afternoon coming back with a sickening clarity. She had managed to avoid thinking of them since getting back to Deanston House, because she had deliberately kept herself busy in the library, refused Cal's suggestion that she take the rest of the day off, and left him in the hall when they went in. He had brought her a cup of coffee at four o'clock himself, inquired if she was feeling better, and gone out. His expression had been cool and inscrutable with nothing of the hard mockery she had seen on the hillside.

But it was no use her pretending any more. Lying

down on top of the coverlet, she found her thoughts and fears washing over her. It was obvious he suspected her – but in what way? He had said – she struggled for some sort of order to her thoughts – what *exactly* had he said? 'I know your name's not Vanessa Collins. So what is it?' She took a deep, shaky breath, shivering slightly as the precise words returned to her – and the memory of his expression came with them. A dark cynical smile on his face, a *knowing* look that had for a moment struck real fear to her heart.

But that doesn't mean he's guessed who I am, she thought, trying to reason it all out. I could be a married woman who's run away from her husband for all he knows. Perhaps that was what he did think. She looked down at her ring finger, with no trace of a mark where a wedding ring might have been. Then on a sudden impulse she got up from the bed, went to her jewellery box on the dressing table, and riffled through it to find a gold dress ring she had always been fond of, one with a plaited design thick and attractive. She put it on and held it away from her to inspect it. That would do. She must remember to wear it all the time now, then *he* wouldn't be able to note the absence of telltale marks. She slipped it off again when she went to wash before dinner.

She made up carefully after changing into a cool long grey dress that clung warmly to her slender figure, making her seem taller and more dignified. Instinct told her that if Cal was going to give her another grilling over her identity, it would be this evening, before her grandfather returned. And it might well be at dinner. And if she looked her best, she would have that extra bit of confidence she felt she needed.

She smoothed silver eye-shadow carefully in, watching herself in the mirror, lips pursed, concentrating. She knew she was beautiful, but the thought was without conceit, for it had not brought her all that much happiness, and she sometimes envied her plainer friends. They had fewer problems – but they would never appreciate that fact, she knew with a wry shrewdness. She sighed, picked up her lipstick and made up her mouth. There, she was ready.

After a last look round the room, Vanessa switched off the lights and went quietly downstairs. She saw Cal sitting in the dining-room – but he was not alone. It was almost a physical shock when she realized that – quickly followed by relief. At least he wouldn't make his insinuations with someone else here. Two women, clearly mother and daughter, were sitting at the table, which was set for four people. Cal looked round, saw her, and stood up.

'Here you are,' he said, almost as if he had been waiting for her. He turned and came towards Vanessa, who took a deep breath, because something had told her that there was hostility in this room and it was directed towards herself.

'Mrs. Macrae, Heather, this is Vanessa Collins. Vanessa, some friends of Mr. Maclean's.' And Vanessa went forward, propelled by the courteous hand on her arm, her thoughts a complete turmoil. No hesitation *now* before the word Collins – and he had called her Vanessa, as if used to it. She had to hold out her left hand, the right being too awkward and sore.

Mrs. Macrae looked at her, light blue eyes shrewd and keen in a beautiful face.

'How d'you do, Miss Collins. How unfortunate that you should have hurt your hand. Is it a little better now?' She wore a flowing dress in some heavy satin material that was an awkward mauve. Vanessa wondered very fleetingly if she knew that the colour didn't suit her a bit. The daughter was different, oh, so very different. As Vanessa turned to her, she knew where the hostility had come from. Heather Macrae was not only a beautiful young woman, she knew it. Her gold-tanned oval face was perfect in every feature, from large limpid violet eyes with thick dark lashes to the sweet curve of pale pink lips. She wore her ash-blonde hair swept back, caught in a matching pink chiffon ribbon that made her seem very young and feminine. Her dress echoed the pink, a filmy affair with low scooped neck and short sleeves. She smiled at Vanessa, and blinked slowly once or twice, and the air bristled with the tension that said: 'Well, I don't like you!'

'Hello,' she said softly, almost shyly. 'Cal—' this with a sidelong, secretive glance at the tall dark man by her side, 'told us about your little accident. How *awful*!' But the meaning behind the words was quite clear to Vanessa, who began to wish she had stayed in her room. They said quite clearly: 'Cal's mine, so watch it – and I'm delighted you were stupid enough to scald yourself.'

'Thank you,' Vanessa smiled back. Such hostility, sudden and unexpected as it was, was always a jolt. But if this young blonde thought Vanessa had designs on Cal, how mistaken she was! And she was already getting practice fending off dislike. Cal was a worthier opponent at least, however unlikeable, than this skinny blonde who was possibly a year older than Vanessa herself, and whose every inch spoke of money and that indefinable air of confidence it carries with it.

Cal walked over to an open sideboard, then half turned. 'What will you have to drink?' he asked. Vanessa saw the glasses in front of the others' places.

'Sherry, please,' she answered. Oh, if he were only always as polite as this! How pleasant life could be. At least he wasn't making his too-accurate insinuations here. That was something. Vanessa would not have put anything past him.

Then Mrs. Banks came in with soup, and the next few minutes were spent settling in, unfolding immaculate white damask napkins. And then Vanessa realized. Of course! Mr. Maclean should have been here by now. Obviously the visitors had expected to have dinner with him and Cal. The conversation during the following few minutes confirmed her assumption, as Cal and the two women talked while Vanessa listened. She had already decided inwardly to behave quietly, more or less wait until she was spoken to before adding her own comments to the conversation. For she was the stranger here, an employee too, and the others obviously knew each other well. She smiled to herself at the idea as she bent to her soup. If only they knew the truth! It would be almost worth it to see the supercilious smile wiped from Heather's face.

But Vanessa held her tongue, drank her soup with great care, remembering what had happened on the previous occasion – and looked up briefly from it to see Cal's eyes on her.

Her own eyes widened briefly. What was on his face? For a brief moment she had glimpsed something puzzling. Then it was gone as he remarked,

'The soup isn't quite as hot as it was at lunchtime.'

'No.' She managed a smile. He was making an effort

to be pleasant. It wasn't hard, looking at the other girl, to see why. Clearly there was something going on between them, that much was plain from the way Heather so frequently glanced at him, and the little secret smiles that she made sure Vanessa could see. Cal, in his role of host in the absence of Mr. Maclean, was perfect in his manners and speech. He deferred to the older woman – and it was obvious that she found him utterly charming, for she developed quite a girlish laugh as the meal progressed. Vanessa wondered how soon after the dinner she could decently escape. One thing was sure – they didn't want *her*. And I'm sure *I* don't want to stay with you, she thought, as she carefully cut into a piece of succulent duckling. But escape proved difficult, as it happened. The last crumbs from the cheese and biscuits sat accusingly on the plates, the last glass of wine had been drunk, and Cal said: 'Shall we go to the lounge? Mrs. Banks will be serving coffee in a minute.' There was a murmur of approval from the by now flushed-faced Mrs. Macrae. Heather looked at Cal and smiled, and Vanessa said to him, very quietly: 'Perhaps you'll excuse me?'

Cal's green eyes narrowed on her. 'But you're going to have coffee?'

'No, thanks. The meal was delicious – but I really couldn't.'

He smiled at her slowly. 'We mustn't offend Mrs. Banks. And she will be if she finds an unused coffee cup left afterwards. She prides herself on her coffee, you know.'

Then you can use two cups for yourself, can't you? Vanessa was childishly tempted to reply. But of course she didn't. Instead she said 'May I take it to my room, then?'

'Of course, Cal,' Heather interrupted in her soft sweet voice. 'I'm sure Vanessa must be tired – with her hand, you know,' and she grimaced sympathetically at Vanessa as if to say: Hard luck, dear – but we don't want you anyway.

It's strange, thought Vanessa, as they walked in leisurely fashion along the corridor to the hall, how shrewd Cal is with me – and yet with *her* he doesn't realize at all. How foolish men are, she added mentally. That one has only to flutter those sooty lashes to have him eating out of her hand. Ah well, they're admirably suited to one another. Which should have been a very consoling thought, but oddly enough, was not.

As the two other women went into the lounge, and Cal waited for her to pass him, Vanessa hung back. She turned to him. 'Mrs. Macrae is right,' she said. 'My hand is making me tired. So I'll just say good night and go up. I'm sorry about the empty coffee cup.'

She saw a muscle tighten in his lean hard jaw. For some reason, she realized suddenly, he was angry. That knowledge gave her a slight feeling of satisfaction, enabling her to say, very quickly: 'And in any case I realize I'd only be in the way. There's a good film on television.' And with that she moved forward, looked through into the room where the two women were already seated, said: 'I hope you'll excuse me now – good night, Mrs. Macrae, Miss Macrae.' She didn't look at Cal as she swept past him. But she felt, for one brief moment, as if he might reach out and stop her, as he had done on the hillside that afternoon.

She closed the door to her room, leaned against it, and let out her breath in a long sigh. That was over! And if I never meet Heather dear again, she thought wryly, I shall shed not a single tear. She crossed to the windows and drew the thick curtains, luxuriating in the rich heavy texture as she touched them. She switched on the television set and looked round at the easy chair, wondering if it would be difficult to move. She briefly regretted not waiting for the coffee, and fetching it up with her, but had no intention of going down for it. She would, she thought, rather drink water.

The closing music of a comedy programme filled the air, and names rolled gently upwards as she reached up to unzip her dress – and found that she couldn't. She had zipped it, one-handed, with some little difficulty, but now the hook was firmly caught at the neck, and needed her two hands to free it. For one absurd moment she debated on the chances of getting down unseen to the kitchen and asking the formidable cockney housekeeper for help. She bit back a laugh that wasn't quite a laugh at the thought. No, I'll look around, and find something that will do it, she thought. A nail file? Scissors? The pictures flashed quickly across her mind's eye as she debated and equally swiftly rejected them. The simplest solution of all – to go down and ask Mrs. Macrae – was instantly dismissed. Heather's face would be too expressive for words. No, never that – and then came the knock at the door, and she turned from the easy chair she was just about to move, and called: 'Come in!' Dear Mrs. Banks – Cal must have asked her to bring— 'Oh!' The shock of dismay jerked her upright from her task as Cal walked in carrying a cup and saucer and a plate of green foil-wrapped chocolates. '*You!*'

He put the things down on the mahogany chest of drawers by the door.

'Who did you expect? Laurie?' he inquired dryly, and his eyes had gone darker as he looked at her. 'What are you trying to move the chair for?'

'So that I can watch television.' She remembered her manners. 'Thank you for bringing coffee.'

'And mints,' he added. He walked over and began to move the chair, pushing it easily although it was large and clumsy – and heavy-looking. 'Say just where.'

'Oh. There – yes, that's it. Thank you. I – er – thought you were Mrs. Banks—'

'Yes?' he lifted one dark eyebrow. 'I'm sorry you were so disappointed.'

'Only I—' she swallowed – and some of her pride had to go with it. It was now or never. 'Only I can't unzip my dress, and I was—' why didn't he interrupt her as he usually did? Damn the man! He stood there, just watching her with a look of polite inquiry on his face. He's enjoying this, she thought. 'I was g-going to ask Mrs. Banks—' he wasn't going to help her, that was obvious. She swallowed the last remnants of her pride and finished: 'Please will you just undo the hook and first few inches of the zip at the top?'

'Certainly! I hesitated to offer for fear you would misinterpret it.' He walked back to where she waited, and she turned, back to him, seething with silent rage at the undoubted satisfaction he was deriving from the situation. His hands were cool and quick. He unhooked the top, there was a faint pause, then began to pull the zip down. So far – no further. She heard his voice softly, and his breath was on the back of her neck: 'Is that far enough?'

'I don't—' she reached up her left hand to feel, and it encountered his, just for a brief second of contact, but the shock was electric. 'Just a b-bit further, please.' Heavens, what was the matter with her? She was trembling like a leaf. Please go away now, she prayed, and felt the zip freed a little more.

'Yes, that's it. Thank you.' She turned, too quickly, for fear he would try and unzip it – although of course he wouldn't – and they collided, and he put his hands on her arms to steady her, and just for a moment time stood still. Tension throbbed, the room seemed suddenly filled with a kind of awareness that was utterly timeless . . .

'Well, I must go and rejoin my guests.' The spell rudely shattered and broke into a million pieces round them, and Vanessa moved away, and Cal turned and went towards the door, and an announcer came on, telling them in a dark brown voice about the film which would follow the news. The door opened, Cal paused, looked back at Vanessa, said: 'Good night,' and went out.

She picked up a cushion from the chair and flung it at the door. And she might have imagined the laugh that came faintly from outside. She stood there perfectly still, breathing hard. But she wasn't angry. The emotion that filled Vanessa was a strange new one to her. It was frightening – and not a little exciting.

She had thought she would go to sleep early. After undressing and sitting in the easy chair sipping her coffee and eating wafer-thin icy mints covered with chocolate, Vanessa felt tired, and decided that after the film she would switch off and get into bed. Yet as it progressed, she found herself increasingly alert. She was listening for sounds from downstairs, but she didn't know why.

What were they doing now? Talking? Playing cards? As the commercials came on, providing an almost welcome diversion in a film that was proving to be not only uninteresting but downright boring, Vanessa went to the window and lifted a corner of the curtain to one side. A sleek grey Rolls was parked at the front outside the porch. And who drove it? she wondered. Mother or daughter? They were still here, at any rate.

In sudden impatience, Vanessa let the curtain fall into place, switched off the television, and went to her bed. She lay awake for ages, gradually being more troubled by the pain in her hand until, unable to stand it any longer, she went to the bathroom and swallowed two of the small white pills from the doctor. Padding silently back across the shadowy room, she heard faint voices from outside and went to the window. Gently, carefully, she eased the heavy velvet to one side and looked down. Light flooded out from the porch, illuminating the Rolls-Royce, and in that warm pool of gold were standing three figures, Mrs. Macrae, Heather, and Cal. They were talking, and someone laughed, and Heather touched Cal's arm in a curiously intimate gesture, then he bent his head, as if to listen to private words, and Vanessa could not have moved away at that moment, not for anything, although she wanted to.

Then Mrs. Macrae waved, and Cal opened the back door for her. She was followed by her daughter after a moment during which she turned to Cal and they exchanged a brief kiss. The door slammed, the window slid down, and Heather leaned out to say something, to which Cal responded with an amused laugh. So they were being driven, presumably by a chauffeur. And why not? Vanessa saw the car purr forward, she was about to drop the curtain into place, but paused to watch Cal, sharply outlined against the background of yellow-gold light. A tall figure – had she ever thought he didn't look tough? He did now, a powerful animal, filled with a startling magnetism she could not deny. Then he turned and looked up, suddenly and surprisingly, directly at Vanessa. Just for a second, but he smiled as he turned away and vanished into the house. Her heart was thudding as she let the curtain drop. He had seen her. And what was he thinking now?

She thought she would not sleep, but the tablets had their effect, and soon Vanessa found herself drifting off into strange disturbing dreams, in the middle of which was a face that wavered and changed from that of an old man to a younger, harder one that was disturbingly familiar.

She woke early, lay for a few minutes thinking about the events of the previous day, then had a cold feeling that gradually filled her. She sat up as she realized exactly what it was. Her grandfather would be here in a couple of hours! There was no backing out now, things had gone too far. But over that thought came another, even more disturbing. Cal would be watching her. He suspected her, maybe without even knowing why, except that he sensed something not quite right, and she would have to act with iron self-control and coolness. Would she be able to do just that? As she washed and dressed, she tried consciously to relax. She would need all her wits about her, at least for the next day or so, and she would keep an eye on Cal Grayne, that was sure. The sooner she went down to breakfast the better. An early start in the library would help. The books were proving more interesting than she had thought they would be, and it was odd, she thought, as she brushed her hair. She had only taken this job, of cataloguing the library full of books, as a means to serve her purpose, and she had expected to hate the work. But she didn't. There was a fascination in handling the beautiful books, reading the titles, touching history as it were, for there is nothing more direct than a book for carrying a sense of immediacy from the past. There were also hundreds of old newspapers, Laurie had said, and shown them to her, neatly stacked in a corner cupboard in the library. Some of them dated from the early eighteen hundreds. Vanessa longed to go through them and sort them into date order. They would be valuable, she knew, and wondered if her grandfather realized that fact. She might know – soon.

When she walked slowly down the wide imposing staircase and into the hall, she heard a door open, and hesitated momentarily. Was it him? She had heard a car distantly when she had been washing, but there had been nothing parked in front of the house when she had gone to the window. Suddenly there came over Vanessa a lost, desolate feeling. Was it all worth it?

'Good morning.' The voice sharply intruded as she took the last few steps and turned to face the man who had come from the lounge. Slight relief came as she realized it was Cal. He was dressed very casually in a pair of off-white cotton slacks and white roll-necked sweater. He looked more tanned than usual, hauntingly attractive – suddenly Vanessa knew what Heather saw in this virile animal – and he was smiling. This last fact put her immediately on her guard. But not without reason.

'Mr. Maclean won't be with us for breakfast, I'm afraid, but you'll see him later.'

'I see. Is he back, then?'

'Oh, yes, he's back.' The green eyes seemed darker this morning, almost grey; a trick of the light, but oddly disconcerning, for his gaze was very direct as he stared at Vanessa, and she was reminded of his looking up the previous night, as she had stood at the window. She turned her head away from him, took the last step, and began to walk towards the dining-room. Cal fell into step beside her, his own legs so much longer, the strides more loping, but slowed down to keep with her.

'And your hand? Is it better this morning?'

'Yes, thank you.'

'Does Dr. Innes want to see you again?'

She looked at him then, slowing her steps slightly. They were nearly at the door to the dining-room, and the corridor was shadowy at the point they had reached. 'He said to change the bandage daily, and to let him know if anything was wrong. But I've got good healing flesh. I don't anticipate any trouble.'

'Good. Can you manage the bandage? Want any help?'

'No, thanks.' She moved away from him. For a moment it had seemed as if he was about to touch her arm, and she wanted no contact with him.

Mrs. Banks had excelled herself at breakfast, perhaps due to her employer's return, for he would doubtless be eating the meal in his room if he were tired after his long journey. Vanessa wondered where her grandfather had been. Abroad? Possibly. She knew nothing about any business interests he might have, for on that subject her father had been strangely reticent.

'Can you manage the bacon single-handed?'

His query startled her, and she looked up. 'What? Oh, yes, thanks, I'll manage.' As if I'd let you cut it up for me, she thought wryly, and watch your amusement. No, thanks! She wondered what would happen over the week-end. Would she be expected to work all day Saturday? Hardly. The morning almost certainly, but the afternoon, and Sunday, would be most tricky. She decided she might go out in her car, not too far, for her hand might trouble her. And then she would read, write letters, or watch television in her room. At least there she would be safe from Cal's insinuations – and his cool, level, watchful gaze.

She looked up suddenly and he was looking at her. For a second their glances locked and held in a strange clash. Her breath caught in her throat. What was that she saw in his eyes? Nothing she could understand, certainly. If hostility, it was well veiled – but there was something more besides, and it was an expression she was not used to, for there was nothing of the bemused admiration she was so familiar with, in most men's glances. She glanced quickly down at her plate and prodded a fat mushroom with her fork. She would let him see that he couldn't bother her.

'I'll start in the library straight after breakfast,' she said, and she could look up now, composure regained.

'Will you? That's good. I'm sure Laurie will be along to help you. How is the work getting along?'

'Quite well. He's a big help. And sorting out the books is far more interesting than I'd imagined—' she faltered. What was she telling *him* for? Why bother?

'Yes?' he prompted. A slight twitch at the corner of his mouth was the only indication that he might be starting to smile. 'You find them interesting, do you?'

He had the power to infuriate her just by the inflection in his voice, by the merest expression – and what was worse, he knew it. For Vanessa *knew* he did it deliberately.

'I do. Why not? Books are fascinating,' she answered coolly. 'Or don't you find them so?'

'Oh, indeed I do,' he agreed. 'Especially ones about other countries – as you may find a lot of these are.'

'I'd already gathered that from the ones I've started with,' she answered, forgetting the enmity for just a moment. Really, she thought, occasionally he shows flashes of something very charming. 'And some are so *old*. Quite fragile really.'

'I know. And dusty. I suggest you leave your bandage-changing until you've finished work for the day.'

She looked at her hand. It was a sensible remark. 'I will,' she said.

'And don't do any lifting with your right hand. Not for a couple of days anyway.'

'No. I wanted to ask – do you know what hours I might have to work tomorrow, with it being Saturday?'

He shrugged. 'No. You'll no doubt sort that out with Mr. Maclean today. It's not my province, I'm afraid. But I wouldn't think he'd insist if you wanted the day off, not with you being so new. Have you somewhere you wish to go?'

She looked at him. 'Visiting, you mean? No, I don't know anyone round here. I'd go out for a ride, but to explore the countryside, that's all.'

'Alone?' One dark eyebrow lifted gently. 'After what

happened the other day?'

'I hardly think I'll meet them again, not round here anyway.'

'No, probably not,' he admitted. 'I've never known anything like it in these parts. But you could easily get lost.'

'Is there a map here?' she smiled at him. 'I found my way up from London, believe it or not, all by myself. In fact, I'm quite good at reading road signs and traffic directions,' and she kept the smile on her face just to let him know she wasn't having any nonsense from *him*.

Cal laughed. 'I'm sure you are.' He picked up the coffee pot. 'More coffee?'

'Yes, please.' She watched him pour out the hot black liquid and add milk. Then the door opened and in walked a stranger, in his sixties, a tall grey-haired man.

Vanessa needed no one to tell her that this was her grandfather.

CHAPTER FIVE

FOR a moment the man stood in the doorway, and Vanessa wondered if her face showed the shock she felt. It was like seeing her father, older of course, but everything else was so familiar; the way this man stood, the lean tanned face, deeply lined, the startling blue eyes, bushy eyebrows. Then he spoke.

'Ah, there you both are.' And that too was so familiar that she wanted to go to him, to tell him . . . She had to put her hand on the table to steady herself. Cal was watching her, then he turned and stood up.

Andrew Maclean walked forward towards them. 'Morning, Cal,' and the brilliant blue gaze was directed towards Vanessa. 'Good morning, Miss Collins.'

He was round the table, and Vanessa found herself shaking his hand, heard herself apologizing for it being her left, found her legs were trembling.

'A cup of coffee, sir?' Cal asked smoothly, and pulled back a chair. Andrew Maclean sank into it.

'Ah, yes, a good idea. I've just had one in my room, but I think another wouldn't come amiss.' He had glanced back to answer Cal who was busy pouring coffee into another cup. Then he looked at Vanessa again.

'Well, I'm sorry I wasn't here to greet you when you arrived. I hope Cal has been looking after you, showing you the ropes?'

'Yes, he has, thank you. We – were just talking about the books, and how interesting they are.'

'You find them so? Ah, good. I always say it's better

to work among things you love. Any problems?'

'No, Mr. Maclean.' She would have to say his name – *her* name – some time, the sooner the better, and it was not as difficult as she had feared it might be.

'But you had an unpleasant accident with your hand. I'm so sorry.' It was strange, but she would have sworn the concern in his voice was genuine.

'It was my own fault entirely. I'm sure it'll be fine in a few days – and it hasn't stopped the work.' She had thought she would not be able to talk to him normally either, but she could. She would have found it even easier if Cal had not been there. Cal, the unknown factor, the man who made her feel uneasy – and guilty – and who seemed to derive a certain amount of satisfaction from so doing.

'Laurie is helping Miss Collins,' Cal spoke now.

'Really?' Her grandfather gave a slight smile. 'I must have misunderstood him before. I seemed to think he would be too busy.'

'Yes. Perhaps he found he could manage it after all.' Nothing in Cal's tone gave him away. Slightly dry, that was all – but she knew precisely what he implied, and wished he would go away. Now that the first shock of her grandfather's arrival was wearing off, she was finding herself watching him, trying to see him impersonally, just as she would if he was in fact a complete stranger. It was what she would have to do if she were not to give herself away – until the right time came. And she was not going to think about that yet.

Andrew Maclean began talking to Cal, asking questions about the house, and then he mentioned Heather Macrae and her mother, and Vanessa sipped her coffee and listened.

'They were a little put out at not seeing you, of course, but I did my best to look after them,' Cal said, and gave her a casual, almost smiling glance. She looked coolly at him.

'Ah yes, must phone them later. It was unavoidable, of course, the trouble in Paris meant delays all along the line.' He swallowed the last of his coffee and stood up. 'Well, I must away and do some work. I'll see you later, Miss Collins.'

He went out, a tall man who walked like a soldier. There was silence for a moment, then Vanessa rose. 'I'm going to begin work,' she said. Then a thought struck her. 'What about lunch?' she asked Cal.

He came slowly to his feet. 'Lunch? I'm sorry, I don't follow you.' Oh, yes, you do, she thought, but you enjoy making everything as awkward for me as you can.

'I mean, where shall I eat it? In my room?'

One eyebrow lifted slowly. 'In here, as you have done.'

Vanessa took a slow, deep breath. 'Look, Mr. Maclean's back now. It was kind of you to invite me here when I was new, but I am an employee in this house and I expect to be—'

'An employee? What a delicate way of expressing yourself! Yes, I suppose you are, but does that mean you imagine you should be consigned to the kitchen for meals, or something?'

She felt her cheeks begin to go pink as she fought for calm. What an infuriating man he was! 'I'm sure you know what I mean. You're a guest – you can't possibly appreciate my position.'

'Can't I?' Green eyes narrowed, suddenly cold. 'You may be surprised. No, Mr. Maclean would be quite startled, and possibly even offended, if you suggested eating anywhere else.'

She stood there helplessly. How did you tell a man like this that you didn't *want* to eat with him, because you were frightened? You didn't. You had to put up with it. Without another word she turned, picked up her handbag, and walked towards the door. He reached it first, and opened it, saying: 'Allow me.'

'Thank you.' She walked quickly out, not waiting to see if he followed, intent only on going into that comfortable library and beginning work. Then, and only then, would she allow herself to think about the man she had just met, the man who was her grandfather, and who did not know it.

She closed the door behind her and flung her handbag on to a chair. A clean overall lay beside it and she put this on, then looked around her, wondering if Laurie would come, and when. It seemed so long ago that she had had the minor skirmish with him, but it had only been the previous morning. She wished now that it had not happened. He worked well, and was a good help, but she needed no more complications to add to the turmoil already in her mind. She mentally resolved to quash any attempts at flirtation firmly at the outset. There was enough trouble with Cal and his veiled innuendoes, and the sudden appearance of her grandfather, without her allowing him to add to it.

So it was that when Laurie knocked and walked in about half an hour later she greeted him with a friendly but completely impersonal smile.

'Good morning, Laurie,' she said.

'Good morning.' His eyes went straight to her hand. 'How is it today?'

'A little better, thanks.' She frowned, puzzled. 'You knew?'

He grinned. 'Oh, there's a good grapevine hereabouts, as you'll find out if you stay long enough. That peacock's enough to frighten anyone. Aye, well, you'll be careful wi' it today. I'll do all the carrying that's needed.'

'Thank you. There's quite a lot to do on these books we already have out first. I was rather slow yesterday—' it was much easier to talk about the books to him, like this. Completely impersonal, immersed in the dusty tomes surrounding them, Vanessa began to find another side to the dark man called Laurie. He really did love the books. And he was clearly making an effort to behave correctly, as if he sensed her mood.

The morning passed so quickly that it was a shock when the door opened, and her grandfather came in. Laurie stood and went over to him.

'Good morning, Mr. Maclean. You had a good journey back?'

'Yes, thank you, Laurie. I see you two are busy. Did you not know the time?'

Startled, Vanessa looked at her watch to see that it was past one. And she still needed a wash! 'I'm sorry,' she scrambled to her feet. 'We were so busy—'

'I know, but you must eat, child. Come away now. These will be here when you come back.' And he waited at the door for them.

Laurie picked up his jacket from the chair with an easy, graceful movement, and stood waiting for Vanessa to go out. But the sleeve of her overall caught over her bandage as she took it off, and Laurie leaned forward to help her.

'Thank you.' She was uneasily aware that her grandfather missed nothing. She ran up the stairs as if pursued, washed her face with her unbandaged hand – she was getting quite expert at that – ran a comb through her hair, and went quickly downstairs to find that the two men were half-way through their soup when she went in.

'I'm sorry—' she began. Andrew Maclean lifted his hand.

'No apologies. It is such a delight to meet someone who actually enjoys their work sufficiently to enable them to forget the time.' He looked at Cal. 'What say you, Cal?'

'Yes indeed.' Hard green eyes searched Vanessa's as if mocking her. And then it came out, quite casually. 'Have you done much of this type of work before?'

'No.' She had had her story prepared for at least a week, and now she was going to have to see if it sounded genuine. She felt suddenly sick. Nothing must show. 'I've been a secretary for two years, but I needed a change because of – er – upsets at work.' So far it was the truth anyway, although she had no intention of telling either man just what sort of upsets there had been at work. 'A friend of mine who works at a solicitor's called Murton, Smith and Kimble,' she paused, stumbling slightly over the name, as if unfamiliar with it, 'told me about the gentleman in Scotland, you—' she smiled slightly at Mr. Maclean, marvelling at the ease with which lies were beginning to come out, 'who needed his library cataloguing, and so I applied as I've always loved books.'

'Ah, you know someone working for the solicitors?' Her grandfather put down his soup spoon and broke a crusty roll in half.

'Yes. She's a secretary there. Not a close friend, more an acquaintance.' And that wasn't a lie. Pat Jones was a secretary there, and wouldn't give Vanessa away – even though the information had actually come from Mr. Murton himself, whom she knew far better.

'Did she tell you anything else?' The question was loaded. And Cal was watching her, she knew, even though he didn't appear to be, which was disconcerting, for she sensed that he was finely tuned to whatever she might say.

She told her first direct lie. 'No,' she said. 'I'm sorry, I don't understand. About this job, you mean?'

Andrew Maclean rubbed his cheek. 'No, nothing really. Now tell me, Vanessa – I may call you that, I trust? How do the books seem to you? I mean, is there any deterioration—' She listened to him, and his questions were all sensible, well balanced, concerning the work she was doing, but there was an undercurrent in the room, a feeling of tension, and she thought she knew what it was. Cal was thinking hard. And what questions – and answers – might he not come up with? Whatever they were, he was clearly not going to say them now. No doubt he would bide his time, try to catch her off balance as he had done the previous day. She watched him. She would be more prepared next time. But when would that be? She was soon to find out.

Her grandfather told her later on that same day that she was not to work on Saturday. It was mid-afternoon when he came into the library where she was working alone, Laurie having not returned after lunch. Vanessa was busy listing books, and at first was not aware that anyone had come into the room, so engrossed was she. A slight cough made her turn to see Andrew Maclean watching her with an amused look on his lean, still handsome face. As always when she saw him, she experienced a sudden twinge of dismay, mingled with fear. What if he should guess – before she was ready?

'I'm sorry,' she said. 'Did you want me? I didn't know—' She put her pen down.

'I came in quietly so as not to disturb you,' and he smiled as he said it, and it was so like her father's smile that it caused her heart to lurch. 'And then I stood admiring the efficient way you were going about your tasks.'

Vanessa looked down at the list on the table before her. For the life of her, she couldn't think of anything to say. Her mind had gone a sudden, curious blank. If it was going to be like this for the next few weeks, she would not be able to bear it, she thought.

Andrew Maclean seemed unaware that anything was amiss. 'Tomorrow is yours,' he said. 'And of course Sunday. I am aware that there is not much in the way of entertainment hereabouts, but please feel free to borrow any of the books you might care to look at.' Then Vanessa's mental block cleared, and she remembered.

'There are a lot of very old newspapers in a cupboard,' she began. 'Laurie showed me – I'd like to go through some of those if I may. They fascinate me.' Something happened to Andrew Maclean's strong face. A look of sheer delight came over it, transforming his features. For a moment he seemed almost boyish.

'My God! The papers – oh, yes!' he said. 'They need sorting as well. Do you know, I have some old copies of a paper called the *Oxford Gazette* dating back to 1665! I'd nearly forgotten about them. Well, well,' he shook his head. 'Yes indeed. I would like them putting in order. It must be years since—' and he suddenly broke off, and for a moment there came something almost distressing on his face. There was a brief silence which Vanessa feared to break, for there was sudden sadness in the room, and it reached out and enfolded her, and she caught her breath in her throat, and she knew ...

'Hmm, must be getting old!' The moment passed, and the slight knowledge which might have been Vanessa's passed too, and all was normal again. 'Yes, certainly, just help yourself. If you want any taking up to your room, I'm sure Cal—' He looked round as the door opened, and Cal stood there.

'I was just telling Vanessa she can look at any of the papers she wished. You'd take up any to her room if she needed, would you?'

'Certainly.' Cal looked from Vanessa to her grandfather. 'I'm sorry to barge in, but Mrs. Macrae's on the phone. I've put it through to your study.'

'Thanks.' He strode out, leaving Cal and Vanessa in the library. She turned away quickly, unwilling for him to see her face, for she felt sure that something of what had so recently passed must show, and she needed time to think ...

'Want any taking up now?' The soft deep voice interrupted her.

'No, thank you.' She didn't look round. She heard his movements, and tensed, then, as she was aware of him right behind her: 'Did you want me?'

'No. I was just looking to see what you're doing.' The voice came now from beside her shoulders, and she felt at a disadvantage, sitting as she was. She uncovered the list immediately, lifting her hands away. Then she looked up.

'I'm cataloguing the books, Mr. Grayne,' she said.

He pulled up a chair and sat beside her, and his eyes gleamed mockingly. '*Mr.* Grayne? Don't you prefer Cal?'

'Not particularly. I don't know you, do I?' she answered, quite reasonably, she thought, and wondered again why he always managed to make her feel ridiculously weak whenever he was too near — as he was now.

'But you call Laurie by his Christian name,' he remarked, and began to feel in his trouser pocket.

'So I do.' And she looked directly at Cal Grayne, and smiled very slowly, almost mischievously. For if there was one thing almost sure to raise this man's uncertain temper, it was mention of Laurie Mackenzie — and he really was asking for it. 'But *we* get on well with each other.'

'Ah! And we don't?' Dark eyebrows lifted imperceptibly, cool dark face remained expressionless — as yet.

'Hardly.' She watched him open a cigarette packet, and when he offered her one, she shook her head. 'No, thank you.' Then she added: 'In fact, you seem to go out of your way to be as rude as you can to me.' And I must keep calm, she added inwardly.

'I suppose you're referring to yesterday afternoon?' he said. The lighter flared briefly, shadowing the other parts of his face, giving it a darkly sinister look.

'Yes.' Better take the fight in the enemy camp, for he would undoubtedly come out with something more later. Here in the library, for some reason, Vanessa felt as though she was on secure ground — far more safe, certainly than on that cool sunny hillside the previous day when she had been feeling particularly weak after a visit to the doctor with her hand. 'You were abominably rude to me – especially when I was feeling so – so awful with my hand. You did it on purpose,' she finished.

'Yes, I did.' It was funny, she had expected a denial, not this cool admission. She stared hard at him, knocked slightly off balance. For a moment she could say nothing, then she found her tongue.

'Then it was a foul thing to do!'

'I agree.' He drew on the cigarette, looked round for the ashtray and carefully put it down in front of him. 'But I had my reasons.'

'Oh. And what were they, may I ask?'

'You already know – don't you?' He was quite imperturbable.

Vanessa began to get that awful feeling, as if the situation were getting out of her control. But she had started it – and now she had to go on. 'Do you think I'm some sort of a *thief* or something?'

'A thief?' he tasted the word, as if the idea had not occurred to him. Then he smiled, very slowly. 'No, not that – at least I hadn't thought of it – yet.'

Temper flared. It was the way he said that last word. 'Then what?' She almost spat the words out.

'I don't know,' he answered. 'But I will.'

'Why don't you get out of this room?' she demanded. 'And leave me alone? I don't have to take your insults – I don't have to take anything from you – do you hear me?' She stood up, eyes flashing fire, and looked down at him, and wished she were a man, because he needed someone to teach him a lesson. Perhaps something of her thoughts communicated themselves to him, for he also stood and faced her, only he was still calm, which was strange, because his temper had a low flashpoint too, and he should be flaring up by now, but he wasn't. And now she had to look up to him, a thing she hated doing, with *him*, for his extra inches mocked her, made her feel smaller and, strangely – weaker. 'Go on. Please go. This is the room where I'm supposed to work. I can't with you here.'

'Don't fret. I'm going – in a few moments. You look mad enough to try and throw me out.'

'If I was a man I would!' She was breathing fast, and had to turn away because she couldn't face him any more. Cal Grayne put his hand on her arm, quite gently, and turned her back.

'Tell me,' he said, and she couldn't tell what was in his voice, but it filled her with dismay. 'Would you?'

She lifted her left hand and bent his fingers back so that he released her. 'Don't touch me,' she breathed. 'I don't like *you* touching me!'

'Just Laurie? I see.'

'How dare—' she began.

'Oh, come on! Don't tell me he'd not just kissed you when I walked in—'

'Really!' But the telltale colour was in her cheeks, she knew, and he laughed.

'It was written all over you both. A quick guilty kiss, eh? Well, let's see how this compares.' And before she could move, he put his arms round her, and then the room was blotted out, because he was suddenly near – too near – and then the nearness was overwhelming, and his mouth was on hers, his lips cool – and yet warm with a kind of excitement at the same instant. Gentle, not rough, not what she had expected. And strangely, it seemed as if the kiss would go on for ever – and why was she not struggling? Vanessa realized with horror that she was actually enjoying the embrace. It broke the spell and gave her the strength she needed to push him away.

'You *beast*!' she exclaimed, her hand going to her mouth instinctively to wipe away the kiss – or to prevent him trying again, she was not sure which.

The green eyes were dark, suddenly, and his expression inscrutable. For a throbbing moment of silence they looked at one another, then he turned away and walked out of the room. That was it. He was gone. Vanessa remained standing where she was, and was dismayed to find herself trembling. Shock and reaction made her unable to move for a moment, then she found her limbs again, and sat down. A blank card lay on the table, waiting to be filled in. She picked it up and crushed it in her left hand, and that small movement provided some relief for the tension that filled her. In her mind was the memory of that kiss – and of how she had felt. She had not been dismayed, or disgusted, or anything she would have expected to feel, with him. The kiss had been absolutely terrific – there was no other word to describe it.

'I must be mad!' she said it very quietly. How awful if he knew! How very *awful*. But there was nothing she could do about that now. She should have slapped his face. It would, after all, have been quite a normal female reaction to an unwanted kiss. It wasn't fear of how *he* would react that had stopped Vanessa – it quite simply had not occurred to her. And *that* was even more disturbing.

Determinedly she bent to her task, deciding that the

only thing to do now was forget what had happened. And at least it had had one good effect; he had gone without pursuing his questions any further. They would undoubtedly come again. The problem was: When? 'I'll be ready for you next time,' she said softly to herself. 'I'll be ready all right.' But she wasn't sure if she was just trying to convince herself.

The work was over for the day, and dinner loomed. Vanessa hoped for a miracle, that either Cal or her grandfather would be going out, but nothing of the sort happened, and when she went down it was to see both men apparently waiting for her. They were standing talking, and her grandfather turned round and smiled as she walked into the room.

'Ah, there you are. I was just saying to Cal—' he paused, his glance travelling swiftly down the grey dress she wore. 'You look very nice. You'll have a drink, Vanessa?'

'Thank you. Yes, please. May I have a sherry?'

'Certainly. Cal?' But Cal was already moving towards the drinks cupboard, putting his glass down on the top, and Vanessa watched him, because she couldn't help herself. What would there be in his glance when he looked at her? She would soon know, for he was filling the glass; it was done. He was turning, coming back towards her with the glass held out – now passing it to her. And he was completely impersonal. Nothing showed on his face. There was not a flicker of anything that she could have taken objection to, merely a polite, casual expression as he said: 'Is that enough?'

'Yes, thank you.'

He inclined his head, so slightly that she might

almost have imagined it – but she knew she had not. There was the merest trace of a mocking glint in those green eyes – just for an instant, before he turned to speak to the older man. And then Mrs. Banks came in with the trolley, and they all moved towards the table, and the moment passed. Just for a second, though, Vanessa had known what his thoughts were, and her fingers tightened on the glass before she put it down on the table. If – if only he were not there, how much easier her self-appointed task would be. But he was, and by the looks of him, at the house for a while. And the sooner she adjusted to that fact, the better, she knew.

They sat down and began the meal; the conversation was general, and quite pleasant, and Vanessa thought how different things could have been if she were a genuine employee, and not who she was. For she was enjoying cataloguing the books, and the house was beautiful and comfortable. But the die was cast. She was here, and she would continue her role, because she had made a promise to herself, and to her dead father. She looked up with a smile on her face, to answer a question from Cal Grayne, and nothing of her feelings showed as she listened to him ask her if she had decided what she was going to do over the week-end.

The meal passed, and all the time, without being aware of it, Vanessa had observed her grandfather, the way he spoke, the way he acted. She was trying hard to reconcile the mental picture she had acquired of him from her father with the man who sat opposite her. It was not easy. She had imagined a hard, brutal man; this Andrew Maclean seemed to be going out of his way to be nice to her – an employee – even to the extent of expecting her to eat at this table.

Just for a moment, towards the end of the meal, Vanessa caught a glimpse of the other man that he might be. They heard distantly a phone bell, and Mrs. Banks came in to say that he was wanted urgently on the phone. He looked round.

'Who is it?'

'*Said* his name was McWilliams,' and she sniffed, as if to say that if they wanted her opinion, it was a phoney name.

Andrew Maclean's face hardened. For a moment Vanessa caught a glimpse of anger – then it was gone. He looked at Cal, a muscle working in his jaw. Cal quietly: 'Want me to take it?'

'No.' The answer was brief, monosyllabic, almost barked, and her grandfather strode out of the room. Vanessa looked down at her plate, speared a sliver of cheese, then, slowly, unable to prevent herself, looked up at the man across the table. He was watching her, his expression quite unreadable, and her heart fluttered in sudden unreasoning panic. She never knew what to make of him when he looked like that. There was a depth to him that was unnerving, she had already sensed this a while back, after first meeting him. She felt the pulse beating at her throat, and said the first absurd words that came into her head: 'Why are you looking at me?'

'Can I not?' Softly spoken, the words mocked her.

'You stare,' she answered. 'I don't like it,' and she tilted her chin.

'There are a lot of things you don't like about me. It's unfortunate, but you'll have to learn to put up with it – if you stay.' The faintest emphasis on the word 'if' spoke volumes.

Vanessa lifted her eyebrows. 'Oh, I'm staying all right. As long as my work's satisfactory – and I'm sure it is. At least Mr. Maclean isn't grumbling, and *he's* my employer.' And that should shut you up, she thought.

Cal smiled. 'I'm sure your work is perfect – from what I've seen anyway. I'm very impressed. But then I think you know *exactly* what you're doing.'

Her grandfather walked in as he finished the sentence, so that the words hung there for a moment before they sank in. But it wasn't until much later that Vanessa remembered them, and their slightly sinister undertones.

Mr. Maclean looked at Cal, and seemed about to say something, but made an almost visible effort to control himself. Vanessa sensed his anger – sensed too that if she had not been there, he and Cal would now be talking about the unknown caller. She looked at her watch, then up. They had nearly finished eating. She wanted to get away, to leave the two men alone to talk – and she knew too that they wanted her to go.

And when, a few minutes later, she asked them to excuse her, there was no argument made. She ran up to her room quickly, quietly, and when she was in it she remembered Cal's remark about her knowing exactly what she was doing. He had not been referring to her cataloguing, she knew that. How she disliked him!

The week-end passed pleasantly. On Saturday Vanessa took a map that had been carefully marked for her by her grandfather and found an enchanting village tucked away at the edge of a loch, and spent an afternoon watching children play in a small playground that had a background of shingly beach and fishing boats. Tired yet refreshed for the change, she returned to Deanston House in time for dinner, then watched television with her grandfather. She would have preferred not to; but was given no choice, and although she felt terribly uncomfortable at first, the feeling soon passed, and it was quite a surprise when Mrs. Banks brought in coffee, and Vanessa saw that it was nearly midnight.

Cal had gone out immediately after dinner. She had been up in her room for her bag and heard his car roar off down the drive. Slowly she had let the curtain fall back into place. She wondered if he was going out with the beautiful Heather. Most likely he was. Vanessa wondered quite suddenly if he kissed *her* in the same way as he had herself. Angrily she turned away from the window, picked up her bag, and marched out to go downstairs. What an absurd thought to have!

She was lying in bed when she heard the familiar note of the Jaguar coming up the drive. Pale moonlight slanted in through one open curtain, and faintly showed the clock face. Ten past one. And Vanessa discovered to her surprise that she had been waiting for just that sound. Now that she had heard it, and knew he was home, she could go to sleep. And she did.

The next few days were busy ones for both Vanessa and Laurie. As she got more immersed in the books, she found her thoughts too occupied to worry about the impossible Callum Grayne. Her feelings about her grandfather were mixed. She had caught glimpses of this other side of him – the one that matched up with her father's descriptions – yet for most of the time his manner was that of a naturally kind person. She was beginning to feel somewhat confused inside. If only there were someone she could confide in, and ask advice. Occasional waves of something approaching regret washed over her, yet there was nothing she could do about it. The only person who knew why she was there at Deanston House was in London – and she was unlikely to get much sympathy from him. Mr. Murton disapproved of what she was doing; he would doubtless advise her to leave – or admit to her deception before it went too far. But it had already gone too far, she knew. Too far to back out.

She was returning two particularly old books to the shelf, and she paused, as a lost desolate feeling swept over her. It was Friday afternoon, a bleak cold day, quite unlike the previous ones, and rain hung in the air like a mist, but was not ready to come down. Laurie had been helping her in the morning, as he usually did, and she almost wished he were back.

They had established a kind of pleasant relationship in little over a week of working together. Vanessa wasn't sure if she could trust him; she sometimes caught him looking at her in a way she knew only too well. Yet strangely it no longer mattered. She could cope – she had learned that at an early age, she had had to, and she wasn't remotely interested in him as a man. She resolutely put a sudden thought of Cal out of her mind. Cal, who was always there, and who watched her without seeming to. Unnerving, that, because he was subtle with it – but she was already so terribly aware of him that she knew, she *knew*, all the time.

He walked in the room at that precise moment so suddenly and quietly and on the heels of her thoughts that she dropped the books.

'Tsk, tsk!' He came forward and picked them up.

'Mustn't let the boss see. These are old.' He handed them to Vanessa, and she took them from him.

'Thanks.' She half turned away. 'If you hadn't crept in I wouldn't have dropped them.'

'Was I creeping?' He looked down at his shoes, soft canvas-topped ones in a fawn shade that echoed his trousers and shirt. 'Perhaps I should wear my climbing boots when I come in here. They clump a bit – but at least you'd know I was about. Is that what you'd prefer?'

'Don't be ridiculous.' She reached up to lift down a book, but it was rather high up, tall as she was, and Cal must have seen, for he too reached up, said: 'This one?' and then handed it to her.

'Your hand's better.' He said it as she took the book from him, using her right hand.

'Yes, it is. There's a red mark, but it'll fade.'

'It will, in a week or so. You can have your first lesson in self-defence now, can't you?'

She couldn't resist it. She didn't intend to, but out it came. 'So that I can protect myself when people like you kiss me?'

Cal Grayne laughed. His teeth were white, not too even, but strong and good, and his face was transformed; even his eyes were laughing. 'That's a thought,' he admitted. 'I'll have to watch it, won't I?'

She was wearying of the discussion. She was uneasy, although she didn't care to admit it to herself, so she moved away as if she had lots of things to do. 'I'm afraid I'm busy at the moment,' she said. 'I really must get on—'

'And scared?' It was softly said, but it made her stop in her tracks.

'Of you?' She smiled her best smile. 'Not at all.' They were watching each other, and tension spread around them, almost as tangible as the grey mistiness outside, and in a minute he would bring up the subject of who she was again – and she wasn't quite ready for it, so she said quickly: 'If you want to teach me, all right, I accept.' And she shrugged. 'But I don't see why you should be so insistent.'

'I saw your face as you walked towards my car last week. You hadn't a clue, had you?'

'All right, I was frightened, of course I was. But—'

'And you'll be less so when I've finished with you. When? Tomorrow morning?'

'Aren't you busy?' she asked sweetly. 'I mean – Saturday?'

'Nothing that can't wait,' was the smooth answer. 'Right, I'll see you down in the gym about an hour after breakfast.'

'What shall I wear?' Despite everything, she was intrigued.

The merest trace of a smile touched his face. 'You can wear the *judoka* if you really wish – that's the judo outfit, there are several in the gym. I'll bring you one up in the morning. It'll save wear and tear on your own clothes. But you must wear a sweater underneath in any case.'

'All right.' She put the books on the table. 'May I get on with my work now?'

'Yes. I came in to tell you that your – employer is going out to dinner tonight, and so am I. He asked me to ask you if you would like your dinner in your room.'

'Yes, of course.' She had detected that slight hesitation before the word employer, and just for a second there, it had seemed – almost as if he had been about to say something else. But what? What could it have been?

Not – her mind refused to take her any further. He could not possibly guess anything else. Could he?

But whatever was in his mind he wasn't going to pursue it further, for he nodded, said 'Right,' turned and went out. Vanessa stood looking at the door. She caught her lower lip in her teeth for a moment. What had she let herself in for? She would soon know.

Saturday morning dawned bright and sunny. The previous day's dullness was blown away as though by a breeze. Vanessa woke up and wondered why she felt anxious. Then she remembered – Cal Grayne was going to give her a lesson on how to look after herself. Knowing him even only slightly, as now, she suspected everything he did. What motives were behind the offer? As she washed and dressed ready for breakfast the question teased her. She must be prepared for any awkward questions, she knew, for they would presumably be alone together in the gymnasium for at least an hour.

She dressed in a plain white sweater and navy blue trews, slipped sandals on her feet, and left her long dark hair loose. A touch of lipstick and she was ready. It was only eight-thirty when she went down to the dining-room. Early – because she wanted to breakfast alone if possible, but Cal Grayne was there, apparently nearly finished, when she went in.

'Good morning,' he greeted her.

'Good morning.' She helped herself to toast and sat down, and he lifted his eyebrows.

'No bacon and eggs?'

'I'm not very hungry.'

'Not nervous, are you?' His tone held solicitude.

She looked coolly at him. 'Nervous? No. Should I be?'

'Of course not. But you seem a little – forgive me – distraite.'

'It must be your imagination,' she rejoined very carefully, for his eyes held that glint she thought she had come to recognize. 'But I would have thought it wise not to eat too much before exercise.'

'True. What a sensible attitude. That's why we're leaving it for an hour.'

'Well then,' she smiled at him, wondering when she had disliked a man so much before. 'You mentioned this outfit. Please don't trouble to bring it up. I'll change in the gymnasium. There is a changing room down there, isn't there?'

'Two, actually. Fine, I'll put one out for you. If you'll excuse me now?' And he stood up and put his chair back under the table. 'Mr. Maclean won't be in for breakfast. He's had to go out early. I'll see you about—' he glanced at his watch '—nine-forty-five, downstairs.'

'Yes.' She watched him leave. When he had gone she poured herself out a cup of coffee. Why on earth had she been foolish enough to accept his challenge?

At nine-forty precisely, Vanessa walked down the stairs to the basement. Inside her, a flutter of excitement, on her face calmness, a giving-nothing-away expression. Whatever happened, she must not let Cal see her inward unease, for that would surely please him. Now there was no backing out, and she almost faltered at the door of the gymnasium at the thought. Once inside, and she would have to go through with it. She reached out and touched the door handle, then walked in.

There was no sign of Cal Grayne; everything was silent, the mats waiting neatly on the floor. Vanessa skirted them carefully as she walked across to the changing rooms. At the doorway she paused and turned back momentarily, for it seemed as if a sound had come from the outer door. It wasn't repeated, and she turned round again to cannon straight into the man who was just coming out of the doorway. He reached out to steady her, this big man dressed as she had never seen him before, in the white judo outfit she had seen so often in photographs and on television but never in reality. The transformation was tremendous. He seemed to have grown in stature, a tall broad-shouldered man, powerfully built, bare-footed, black belt tied at the waist of the loose jacket that was open to show a bare, very hairy chest.

'Oh!' Stupidly, Vanessa tried to pull herself away, stricken by sudden panic. If she could have run away she would – but he was holding her, releasing her only slowly, almost reluctantly.

'It's only me.' The deep voice was amused, the green eyes held hers as if mesmerizing. 'Your suit's in there, the second room. I'd better show you how to tie the tapes round your waist. Off you go.' And he stood aside to let her pass. Feeling almost as if she were going to her execution, Vanessa walked past him and went into the small warm room.

CHAPTER SIX

'I'VE changed my mind. Let's not bother.' The words were there, but they remained unspoken as Vanessa faced Cal Grayne on the mat opposite each other. *Tatami* matting, made from the straw that is left after the rice is harvested, he had told her, and it had the give of a good carpet – but she didn't really care. She looked down at herself, and knew now why he had told her to keep a sweater on, for the jacket was loose, even though well belted. As he had tied the tapes for her – a very personal, rather disturbing touch, that – he had told her that jackets were often wrenched nearly off, although, he had added with what could have been a grin, she had no need to worry about that – yet . . .

He had changed, in a way that she found difficult to define. He seemed a different person, calmer, assured in a manner quite unlike his usual one. He looked at her, then spoke. 'First, before we do anything, we have to warm up, to get your muscles ready for action. I want you to watch what I do, and follow, okay?'

'Yes.' Vanessa passed her tongue across her dry lips. She must concentrate, she knew. After all, looking at it from a purely practical viewpoint, this could be of real use to her, and he was taking the trouble to do it – for whatever reasons – for which she should feel gratitude. So she watched him, finding the loosening-up actions easy to follow, gradually feeling the tensed muscles of her body become easier, especially the forward rolls, with her body curled into a ball – which she had thought might be difficult but weren't – and no doubt this was what he had intended.

'Stop now. That's enough.' He came over to her. 'Stand quite relaxed. There, that's it – no, your neck's stiff – *relax* it.' His touch was firm yet gentle – and quite impersonal. Vanessa moved her head in response to the mild pressure of his hands, heard him say: 'That's better. Now, before I teach you anything, you should know how to fall, so that you won't hurt yourself.'

'I see.' It was most odd. He had taken his hand away, but the impression of his warmth remained. She took a deep breath, seeking for calm, wishing she could feel as truly relaxed as she should. How much easier it would all be if only she could forget her suspicions of him, and concentrate ...

'Are you listening, Vanessa?'

'I'm sorry?' Pink-cheeked, she looked at him, but his regard was quite impersonal. And then she knew why he was different. The aggression, the prickly atmosphere, all were gone. He spoke calmly, coolly. And that was the moment she began to really relax.

'Lie down. I'm going to show you how to fall. No, wait. I'll do it first.' The next second he was on his back on the mat, down with one fluid, almost graceful movement. 'Now watch. You practise like this at first, then you crouch and eventually stand – and you'll find, if you learn it properly, that you can fall without hurting yourself.'

Vanessa watched him. There was a fascination about this man anyway, at the moment, and she wanted to see exactly what he did, because suddenly, surprisingly, it was important that she became a good, attentive pupil. And so she noted his movements, the way he rolled to his right, his straightened arm from shoulder to fingertips, beating down on the mat at the same instant, his legs drawn up. There was a look of concentration on his face, but he was speaking softly all the time, telling her that this was the sideways breakfall – the *Yoko Ukemi* – that the Japanese terms were used in judo throughout the world, so that in international contests, even if people spoke only their own languages, there was instant understanding.

Then he was on his feet. His voice had an hypnotic quality. When he said: 'Right. Lie down, your turn now,' Vanessa obeyed instantly. He crouched beside her.

'That's it. Arm straight – *straight*. Right. Now do what I did.'

She only felt foolish for a moment. There was something so abstract, so completely impersonal about Cal now that he was a cool dark stranger, purely a teacher – and a good one. For with every movement, every word and touch of assistance from him, she found her body responding. She wanted to do it right. She really did.

Then suddenly he stopped her. 'That's enough. Now let's do the next stage. Think you're ready?'

'Yes, I think so. Is – is it all right so far?'

'Not bad,' was the laconic reply. She sensed approval, although she could not have said why – but it was enough.

He made her repeat the breakfall, first from a squatting position, tucking her chin closer in, touching, helping her, and all the time in this quite impersonal way, and then from a greater height.

'All right, we'll take a break now. Go and sit on the mat. I'll show you a few other falls while you take it easy for a moment. You must never overdo it – you must tell me if you get tired or achey at all. You understand?'

'Yes, I understand.'

But although she watched him intently for the next few minutes, it wasn't what he was doing that really registered. He had explained briefly before starting that he wouldn't be teaching her any different falls yet, just the one, but there was no reason why she shouldn't see them practised. There was a graceful quality to his movements, and she found herself fascinated. She couldn't have repeated what he did, she knew that, but then he wasn't trying to teach her them anyway. It was the man himself who intrigued her. He was so different, so very different. Not just the clothes, although they were startling enough to her eyes, his whole manner had changed in a way that made her feel – albeit reluctantly – respect for him. He knew *exactly* what he was doing. And more, he was managing to convey it to Vanessa. She had felt the confidence, after the first few seconds on the mat, felt the clarity of direction emanating from him – and been able to obey his most precise instructions.

She came back to the present as he stood. 'Ready?' he said. His hair was untidy; a lock fell over his forehead and she had to stop herself from brushing it back as he reached out to pull her to her feet. A sudden impulse that made her bite her lip in dismay. What would he think of that? The idea was nearly funny.

'Tired yet?'

She looked at him. Faint perspiration beaded his forehead. The gymnasium was warm. Vanessa longed for a drink of water, but dared not ask. 'No – only a little,' she admitted. 'But it's nothing.'

Cal smiled very slightly. 'You mustn't get tired. You

must say. There's no point in trying to learn if your muscles are protesting, you know. It takes time.'

'Yes, I'm sure. You're very good.' She hadn't intended to say it, but it came out before she could think about it.

'Thanks. I started when I was very young, though.'

'You're a black belt.' It wasn't a question, for he was wearing it.

'I am. Mr. Maclean's a brown belt – he's damn good too, for his age.'

'Is that why you're here? To teach him?'

'No.' He shook his head faintly. 'Not at all. I'm a guest, my father was a good friend of his years ago. I'm doing some – writing,' he hesitated slightly before the word, 'while I'm here. And of course the odd judo session.'

Vanessa turned her head slightly away before her expression could show her thoughts – but she had forgotten he was practically a mind-reader. She found his fingers on her chin, propelling her face back, so that their eyes met in a gentle clash as he spoke softly: 'Go on – say it.'

'Say what?'

'What you're thinking – that I'm some sort of sponger, just idling my time away here—'

'Don't be ridiculous!' She tried to make her voice confident, for the last thing she wanted was an argument with him. Not now, not at the moment. They were doing so well. A shame to spoil it . . .

'I wouldn't blame you if you did.' He had the constant ability to surprise. As he was intending to now. 'It's just what I'd think. But I am working – on a book.'

'Oh, I see. A novel?' She didn't really want to know. The less they trespassed on each other's private lives, the better – for in a minute, knowing him, he would be getting on to *that* subject again, the last thing she wanted. But it would have been almost impolite not to ask.

'No. About travel. I've just come back from a journey across Europe. I'm getting it down on paper.'

'Oh.' She wanted to begin the lesson again. His words about the book weren't really registering, for all she could think about now was keeping him off the subject of why *she* was at Deanston House. Much later, she would recall them. 'C-can we do some more?'

'Certainly. Now you've learned how to fall – and quite well, I might add, for a total beginner – we'll do a bit more together. I'll throw you–' he stopped at her almost imperceptible flare of alarm, and laughed. 'Not properly – I'll stop the fall just before you land. You'll see. It's an extension of what you've been doing alone.'

They faced each other, each lightly gripping a lapel and sleeve as she had been shown. 'Keep a firm grip, whatever you do, and trust me.'

Suddenly, almost imperceptibly, she felt the grip tighten as his body began to turn. He seemed to pivot on his toes and almost at once Vanessa felt her balance start to go. Then Cal's right shoulder was beneath her arm, his body seemed to go into a tightly coiled crouch and in a single movement, graceful in its fluidity, she felt herself drawn forward over his shoulder.

For a moment of blind panic, she felt herself lose all contact with the ground, and then – a gentle pull completed the move and she was rolling forward on her shoulders like a ball, hardly aware that she had made contact with the ground. As she came upright, Cal was grinning at her from a crouched position. It was an odd, strangely enjoyable sensation, she discovered to her dismay, for although he held her impersonally, yet there was something . . . And how very strong he was . . .

'Again? That wasn't too bad, was it?'

'No.' She had to take a deep breath. 'No. I thought I was going to go f-flying,' but that wasn't really why she was stammering – although she had no intention of telling him *that*.

'I told you to trust me.' He sounded almost amused. 'You don't think I'd have really let you fall hard, do you?'

'I don't know what to think about you.' She hadn't intended to say it, and regretted it instantly. But it was too late. His expression changed only fractionally, his eyes narrowed. Then he smiled.

'I know you don't. The feeling is mutual. I don't know what to think about *you* either.'

She wanted to get well away from him. She put her hand to her forehead. 'How l-long have we been down here?'

'Nearly an hour. Why? Had enough?' He was watching her, seemingly casual, yet there was this brittle tension building up again, this tension that so frightened her, for she was unable to dispel it.

'I – my legs feel a little shaky,' she admitted, not needing to lie, for they were.

'Then we'll stop. I told you to tell me when you felt tired. We'll have another lesson tomorrow. It will be good, so soon after this one – you'll pick things up more quickly.'

For a moment Vanessa wondered how she could get

out of it. Then she realized – better to agree now – there would be time later to think up a good excuse if necessary. He was too keen-eyed to deceive – at this moment especially, as she was in a state of tiredness.

'Yes, thanks. Tomorrow will be fine.'

'In the afternoon. About three?'

'Y-yes. I'll go now. I'll change upstairs, in my room.' The sooner she got away the better. 'I'll let you have the suit back later on.'

'Keep it for tomorrow,' was the reply. 'You'll really need it then.'

'Thank you for the lesson,' she managed, and began to walk towards the changing rooms for her trews and sandals. He followed her.

'A pleasure.' But the words could have been sarcastic – she couldn't be sure of anything any more. His touch had been disturbing before, during the time he had been teaching her; perhaps more so because she knew it had all been quite impersonal on his part.

She waited until he vanished into the other changing room, and then fled.

Nobody had told her that Heather and her mother were coming for dinner that evening, and Vanessa felt a stab of sheer dismay as she walked into the dining-room to see the laughing group standing by the window, drinks in hands. The image was imprinted on her brain, the tall men, Cal leaning slightly forward to hear something that Heather was saying quietly to him, her grandfather handing Mrs. Macrae a glass. There was a completeness about the scene Vanessa hesitated to break, for she felt suddenly as an intruder would – unwanted – and wished she could have gone away. But it was too late. Cal must have ears like a hawk, for he half turned.

'It's Vanessa,' he said, and looked across at her. Her grandfather turned too.

'Come in, come in. You've met Vanessa, hey, Anne?'

Mrs. Macrae gave the advancing Vanessa a very gracious smile.

'How are you, my dear?'

'I'm fine, thank you, Mrs. Macrae.' Vanessa gave her a warm responding smile. She was much nicer than her daughter. How sad that she had no idea about clothes. Her long dress was even more unfortunate than the maroon one, being a bright yellow that drained all the colour from its wearer's face. Her grandfather seemed keen enough, however. His regard was warm as his eyes rested on the woman at his side, and Vanessa thought, with a sudden stab of realization: He's in love with her. It was an odd feeling, knowing that. And was Cal in love with the daughter? Was that one reason why *he* stayed? Vanessa accepted the glass of sherry with thanks, and found her eyes on the couple outlined against the window as she sipped her sherry. Hard to tell. She imagined a man such as Cal would hide his feelings very well if he chose to – and there was nothing in his manner now to suggest anything save warm friendliness towards the beautiful girl he was talking to. She saw him light a cigarette for her, saw Heather's hand touch his, holding the lighter, the gentle personal caress that lasted only for a few brief seconds. Vanessa turned away quickly, and heard her grandfather say:

'Well, Vanessa, how did your lesson go today?'

The question fell into an almost visible silence. It seemed as if Heather tensed. Ridiculous, of course, but

Vanessa sensed the listening quality in the air, and what on earth could she say that wouldn't antagonize the beautiful blonde even further? How she wished she were not here!

'Very well, thank you. I felt a little stiff afterwards for a while, but it seems to have passed.' And please let's change the subject now, she added inwardly.

'Why, Andrew, what lesson was this?' Anne Macrae said in her clear, high, carrying voice.

Andrew Maclean laughed. 'Cal thought Vanessa needed some lessons in self-defence, so he took her to the gym this morning for a judo session.'

Mrs. Macrae turned slowly to Vanessa, whose heart sank. Too late now.

'Really? How fascinating!' But the voice was a shade less warm than before. 'Tell me, did you find it difficult? I mean, isn't it a bit *rough*?' And she wrinkled her nose in faint distaste.

'Well, I was learning how to fall at first, so that was quite easy.' Then Vanessa saw the expression on Heather's face, the deep dark fury in those beautiful eyes, and something happened. She had nothing to lose. She hadn't started the conversation – and Heather already loathed her. 'Then Cal taught me something very different, which involved throwing me – only he didn't let me fall hard, it was very pleasant really.' And Vanessa turned to him and smiled. She didn't know what was coming over her – she would definitely have to think about this later, but just at the moment she really didn't care!

Cal nodded; his face was giving nothing away – yet. 'It was a fairly simple fall. You soon got the hang of things.'

'You're an excellent teacher.' Vanessa sipped her sherry. They were all looking at her, her grandfather with an expression of benign interest, Mrs. Macrae fairly shrewdly, Heather with frank loathing, and Cal – what was it about Cal? He seemed almost to be enjoying himself.

'And so strong.' And she smiled at Heather very nicely. Let her think what she wants about *that*, she thought, with a slight feeling of cat-like satisfaction – and if I'm any judge of character, she added inwardly, Cal's in for trouble later. Oh, what the hell, here goes. 'He sort of lifted me,' she looked at her grandfather as she spoke, but the words were for the benefit of the beautiful Heather, 'and then threw me – only he had hold of me all the time, and I landed very gently. It was a very odd sensation – almost frightening – only I wasn't scared.'

Andrew Maclean threw his head back. 'Oh, I should have been there!'

Heather spoke then, very casually, but Vanessa heard the tautness behind the words. 'Why, Cal, you've never told me about this,' there was ever such a pretty pout to her mouth. 'I never knew you were a judo expert.'

'I didn't think you'd be interested, my sweet,' he answered teasingly. What a different man from the cool dark judo instructor of hours before!

Mrs. Banks clattered in with the dinner wagon loaded with plates of smoked salmon, a huge dish of fluffy omelette, and they drifted to their places, and Vanessa felt reaction set in. How stupid to rise to the bait of Heather's dislike. What did it matter? And there was the rest of the evening to get through. She would go to her room immediately after dinner, she decided, as she forked up the first bite of succulent smoked salmon, lightly sprinkled with fresh lemon juice. And that was surprisingly easy. When she told her grandfather that she would like to be excused, as they made their way to the main lounge after the delicious meal, he agreed quite pleasantly. Vanessa thought she knew why. Anne and Heather Macrae were his good friends – the mother particularly so – and the daughter's dislike was overt. He wanted no trouble.

But yet there was a faintly sad feeling in Vanessa as she went up the stairs, and when she reached her room loneliness came over her. The image of the little group as it had first been when she had walked into the dining-room nearly two hours previously remained with her. She had been the outsider, the newcomer – not wanted.

There were books to be read, and television to watch, but neither appealed, and after half an hour during which she alternately watched the antics of an American detective, and glanced at the spy thriller on her knee, Vanessa stood up and switched off the set and closed the book. She suddenly remembered the newspapers in the library. She had permission to go through them – so why not now? An hour would pass very quickly, and then she could go to bed, for faint muscular twinges were a constant reminder of the judo lesson, and she certainly would not sleep if she went now.

Vanessa opened her bedroom door and listened for a moment before crossing to the top of the stairs. Soft lights gleamed, lighting the landing and hall below, and faint laughter and voices and the chink of glasses came from the lounge. Nobody would hear her now if she went down. Not that it mattered if they did...

She switched on one light in the vast shadowy room,

and walked surefootedly to where she knew the papers were. She lifted the box down carefully, debating whether to carry it up, or just take a few of the ancient newspapers out. There would be a lot to read, a few would do – and yet there would be a fascination in putting them in date order. Before actually beginning to look at them. And that would save time later. The box was heavy, but not much so, and she bent to pick it up, but the room was shadowy, and her elbow dislodged a book which fell on to the carpet with a thud.

'Dammit!' she said it quietly, and put the box down to enable her to pick up the book. Sudden light flooded the room and she turned to see Cal standing in the doorway – and, most oddly, she felt like some criminal caught red-handed.

He walked softly over the thick carpet. 'Well, well, what have we here?'

Vanessa stood up, poise regained after that brief feeling of confusion. 'I decided to take the newspapers up to my room to look at, that's all.' She had avoided looking at him properly before, in the dining-room, but now it was only too easy. In fact it would have been difficult to look anywhere else but at this devastatingly attractive man in dark suit, dazzling white shirt, dark grey tie – a greater contrast than normal because of the way he had been during the lesson, but in any case he looked superb. With the main light behind him his face was in shadow, dark and mysterious, his eyes unfathomable. Vanessa moved, suddenly uneasy, turned away, bent to pick up the fallen book and replace it on the shelf.

'I'll take the box up to your room for you,' he said.

'There's no need. Your friends will be wondering where you are, won't they?' She said it without any attempt at sarcasm, but perhaps it came out that way anyway, for she saw him give a slightly crooked grin as he brushed past her and stooped to lift the box.

'The atmosphere is slightly cool where I'm concerned,' he said dryly. 'Due no doubt to your detailed explanation of the judo lesson.'

The sheer injustice of it took Vanessa's breath away for a second – and perhaps the merest, *slightest* twinge of guilt too? Then she found her voice. 'Well! Of all the damned cheek! It wasn't me who brought the subject up in the first place, if you remember.' Pink stained her cheeks, her breast heaved, and she could not be aware of how excitingly beautiful she was at that moment. She would have been too mad to care even had she known. And she almost forgot just then her feelings at seeing Heather's face, so her indignation managed to sound all the more real . . .

'Now hold it, little wildcat!' Cal sounded faintly amused. He was carrying the box. And Vanessa didn't want to talk to him any more. She turned and went out of the library. Let him bring the box up if he wanted – and if not, the hell with him anyway!

She ran up the stairs as if chased, across the landing, into her room, and paused, listening. Surely he would not come up? He would put the box down, shrug those broad shoulders, undoubtedly mutter: 'The hell with you too!' and go back to his waiting girl-friend in the lounge . . .

'Don't run off next time.' He was in the room, hooking his foot up to slam the door behind him, surveying her in that cool appraising way he had, then he put the carton down on a chair. 'Do you always run off when you're getting the worst of an argument?'

Vanessa's eyes widened. 'Me? The worst – you must be joking! What argument? I simply told you—'

'A nicely balanced version of what happened. Yes – I heard you! Saw your face too – you loved it, didn't you?'

Vanessa stalked towards the door, ready to open it. 'Will you—' but he stopped her when he swung her round.

'No, I won't get out. Not till I'm ready.' He was holding her arm, and although his grip wasn't tight, it was firm.

'Do you always use strong-arm tactics on women who disagree with you? It must help you win a lot of arguments,' she spat out, and pulled. 'Let me *go*!'

'No, I don't, but then most women aren't like *you*, are they? You've got a fine old temper – and it reminds me of someone—'

She froze. Now she knew why he had come. Any minute now, any minute . . .

Anything to create a diversion. *Anything* to stop him getting too near that frightening, forbidden subject. 'Oh,' she moaned, and tears welled up in her eyes, the tears she had had the gift of bidding, without any effort, since childhood. 'My wrist – it – it hurts!'

He released her suddenly, then tilted her chin up and stared hard at the brimming brown eyes. 'My God!' he said softly, 'and a damn good actress too!'

'I don't – I don't know what you mean,' it was coming quite easily now, and as long as he didn't begin again . . .

'Yes, you do!' And he laughed. 'What a woman!' He lightly pinched her chin. 'So long, Sarah Bernhardt. I can't stand tears, as you know. I'll go back to the slightly cooler atmosphere downstairs. No doubt I'll be able to extricate myself more easily from trouble there.' And he gave her a significant smile before turning and going out.

Vanessa stood looking at the door behind him before moving over to the chair on which the box rested. She had a table under the window. After a moment's hesitation she carried the box across to it and began to lift the newspapers out on to it.

There were nearly two hundred of them some in very fragile condition, mottled, the paper almost brown, others soft and thin yet sturdier. There would be a lot of work involved there, but she sensed that in a way it could be more fascinating than the books themselves. Vanessa smoothed a crease out of a copy of *The Times* for 1854, and laid it on top of the pile. The papers had a faintly musty dry smell, and she wondered how long they had lain, forgotten, in their box. She was soon to know...

The two sheets of writing paper were quite near the bottom of the box. At first Vanessa lifted them out without realizing exactly what they were, and was about to put them on one side when she paused, seeing the name that was so often repeated on the top sheet...

Andrew G. Maclean, written at least thirty times down the page, in exactly the same way, like somebody practising... Practising a signature – her grandfather's signature. She picked the top sheet up, to look more closely, and the writing on the second one was revealed. It was like a letter, except that it was repeated half-way down the page, and the top half was scored out. And Vanessa knew she should not be reading other people's letters, but something so disturbing now filled her that she could not put it to one side.

Written on the page was the brief message: 'This is to authorize the bearer, John Maclean, to take cash on the enclosed cheque, also to remove contents of my safety deposit box, no—' But she could read no more. A dreadful knowledge flooded her, the realization of why that careful, practised line of signatures was on the other sheet. She held them side by side. The 'letter' was also signed, with an exact copy of the one on the other sheet. There was no doubt about it – someone had practised Andrew Maclean's signature until it was perfect, and then written a letter of authorization – and doubtless a cheque – and for some reason these practice runs had been pushed into a pile of old papers and forgotten. And who had done it? There was only one answer, only one John Maclean that Vanessa knew. Her father.

Immediately after she rose and dressed the following morning, Vanessa went out for a walk. Breakfast was after nine, or had been the previous Sunday, for her grandfather went to church soon after, but Vanessa had no appetite. The sickening knowledge she now carried was like a heavy weight in her stomach, and left no room for food. She wanted nothing to eat – she doubted that she would ever again. She slipped out of the front door, dressed in a warm red coat, for the air was cold and fresh, and a low mist hung over the lawns and swam round the huge rhododendron bushes. She turned left, hands dug deep in her pockets, head down as she looked at the gravel drive underfoot ahead of her, quite unaware of the man watching her from a window of the house.

She had slept very badly. Shadows under her eyes

emphasized the delicacy of her face, making her seem more pale than usual. The drive split, the part she now took leading round the back of the house, and then down for nearly a mile. She walked along, oblivious of her surroundings, even of where she was going, not seeing the tiny furry creatures watching her, pink noses twitching, before they scampered away.

Vanessa saw nothing, only the burning image of a sheet of signatures – forged by her father – which made him a criminal, in intent if not in fact. Had he gone through with it? And if he had, had he succeeded, or been found out? There was no one she could ask, ever. And she knew now what true torment was, for all her reasons for coming to Deanston House had suddenly crumbled away. Who was to say now that her father had been justified in the things he had told her? So her grandfather had been a hard, unsympathetic man to his only son. Perhaps with good reason? Vanessa paused, her footsteps faltering into silence, so that the mist seemed to rush back round her. Her face felt drawn and tight. She had believed her father's stories of the treatment given him by Andrew Maclean, the strictness with money, the reluctance to let him choose his own marriage partner, other things too, so that in the end he had been forced to leave home to seek a new life. But he had never mentioned forging signatures. Perhaps there were other things he had left out too ... Vanessa remembered the gambling her father was addicted to, the way he had let her pick out horses' names with a pin. It had been fun then, just a game to the child who adored her father, the child who could not understand her mother's tears, or the arguments about money. A clearer picture emerged, quite suddenly, like a jigsaw half completed, so that the remaining pieces are easier to fit. She walked on, as if to shake off the most disturbing memories, and a voice said: 'Good morning. Early for a walk, isn't it?'

She looked up to see Laurie standing in front of her. To the right of them were some grey stone outbuildings, and a courtyard.

'Good morning. Yes, I needed one.'

Laurie frowned. 'Are you all right?'

Alarm flared in her eyes, as if he might read her thoughts. 'Yes – yes, of course. What do you mean?'

'You look pale, as if you've had a shock. I'm sorry for saying it. But if you don't feel well I'll stay with you a bit.'

Vanessa tried to smile. 'Thanks, Laurie. It's nothing. I'll go back in a minute. What is there down the path?'

'Och, nothing much, a small lake, some trees, an old wee house. The path winds round another mile or so, then leads back to the big house round the other side. Will I walk round with you?'

'No, thanks.' She shook her head, and that slight movement made her feel dizzy. Laurie reached out his arm. 'Come away in a minute. There's only my mother. She'll make you a cup of tea.'

The temptation was great, but she didn't want to face anyone else just now. She didn't want to have to make conversation. She just wanted to be alone, to think.

'Thanks, Laurie, but I won't. I'll turn back now. Please don't come. I'm fine, really.'

'Aye, well, I'm going that way anyway. Come on now.' There was to be no getting away from him, that was clear, and the sooner she was in her own room, the better. She smiled at him, a genuine one this time.

'All right, Laurie. But I won't fall over or anything, I promise you.'

He grinned in response to that smile. 'Ach, that's a shame. I'd ha' liked fine to carry you back.' They walked along in pleasant silence for several moments, and the mist lifted visibly, melting into the sun that was gathering strength up in the sky, giving a promise of warmth to come later.

'I'll be there tomorrow morning in the library,' he told her as they neared the house.

'Will you? Good.' She would not mention the newspapers, unless he asked. He might notice they had gone. She had hidden the two sheets of paper under that lining the bottom drawer in her dressing table. Because there *might* be an innocent explanation, and it would never be discovered if they were destroyed ... Even though she *knew*, she had to cling to something ...

'Vanessa?'

'I'm sorry?'

'I said, are you okay now?'

'Oh, yes, I'm sorry. Yes, fine, thank you, Laurie. I'll see you tomorrow.' They were standing at the foot of the steps leading to the front door. Laurie turned away, and she said in surprise: 'Aren't you coming in?'

'Ah, no. I just wanted to see you were all right. Away and have a good breakfast mind. You'll feel stronger.'

'Thanks, Laurie.' She touched his arm, surprised at his solicitude. 'Thank you very much.' She turned and ran up the steps, and opened the door. The wash of unhappiness swept over her as she closed the door behind her, and she stood there for a moment trying to fight it, trying desperately to forget what had happened. But it was no use. This had been her father's home, and

133

it was her grandfather's, and there was no undoing what was done and past. With a deep breath of despair she ran across the hall and up the stairs, across the landing into her room.

She lay down on her bed, and the hot tears flooded out, spilling over her cheeks, scalding them, tasting salty on her lips, and she turned her head sideways into the pillow and let them come.

She never heard the knock on her door, or the voice calling her. She heard nothing until the door opened, and Andrew Maclean walked in. Shocked, startled beyond words, she sat up, seeing him only vaguely through a thick blur of tears at first, not even sure if it was him or Cal for a moment.

Then he spoke: 'My dear child, what is it?' And he came forward to the bed. Vanessa could not speak. No words would come. She just shook her head helplessly. And felt his hand on her shoulder.

'It distresses me to see you crying. What is it? Is it anything we have done? Vanessa, for heaven's sake, child, you'll make yourself ill. Please stop.'

Gradually the sobs subsided as his plea sank in. She took a few deep shuddering breaths. 'I'm sorry. No – it's nothing you've done – really. I can't tell you, I'm sorry. It's very personal.'

He sat down heavily on the bedside chair. 'Then I won't ask again. But please let me help. You've not breakfasted, have you?'

'N-no.'

'Then Mrs. Banks will bring you some up. I insist. Then you must come down and we'll have a nice talk in the lounge, and a cup of coffee.'

'But you go to church!' Vanessa looked at him.

He smiled. 'I can always give it a miss for one week, can't I? I certainly can't go and leave you like this, not knowing, and I would hesitate to ask Cal, for he's busy writing this morning – and besides—' Then he stopped.

'Yes?' she prompted.

He smiled slowly. 'I get the impression that you two manage to strike sparks off each other—'

'Oh!' her shocked gasp of dismay interrupted him, and he laughed.

'Don't worry, my dear, I understand it well. Perfectly normal reaction. Cal is quite an aggressive male – and you give me the impression of being a young woman with a mind of her own – good! I like that! My word, I bet those judo lessons will be something when you're more proficient.'

Despite everything, that thought made Vanessa smile. 'I'm sorry,' she managed. 'I didn't realize—'

'Not at all!' He stood up. 'Think nothing of it. I enjoy young people about me. Now, may I suggest you bathe your face? I'll away down and have Mrs. Banks make up a tray. Then I'll see you in the lounge when you've finished eating.' He turned and walked out, closing the door quietly after him.

Vanessa filled her washbasin with cool water and plunged her face in, opening her eyes under the water, a trick she remembered from years before, for refreshing them. She dabbed herself dry, heard Mrs. Banks' voice calling, and told her to come in.

The tray was laid with a crisp white cloth, a plate of bacon, eggs and mushrooms, fine thin buttered toast, and a pot of coffee.

'Oh, Mrs. Banks, thank you very much,' Vanessa

said.

The housekeeper sniffed. '*He* asked me,' she admitted grudgingly. 'Said you ain't been well.'

'No, I wasn't. But I'll feel better after eating this, I'm sure.'

Mrs. Banks' look implied that she wouldn't be too sure of that, but she nodded. 'Right then, I'll let you get on with it.' And she vanished. Vanessa sighed. She wondered if she would ever manage to get past the woman's prickly reserve. Then she knew – she wouldn't. For she would not be here long enough. She could not stay now, not knowing what she did. All her plans for revenge had melted away, shattered by her discovery of the previous night. She wondered how soon she could decently leave. There was a lot of work to be done yet in the library, several weeks in fact, but she knew she could not bear to stay that long, nursing her secret discovery to herself. Nor could she tell her grandfather the truth. How could she hurt him further? He had presumably got over things years before; it was not up to Vanessa to reopen these old wounds. Better to leave quietly – and never return.

He would soon get over his longing to meet his unknown granddaughter. She pictured telling him who she really was, and shuddered at the thought. How could she ever admit to the shabby deceit she had attempted? To admit that she had planned to tell him exactly who she was – and then walk out of his life for ever? Having met him, she knew it could not be done. Not any more. Not now. It was too late, all too late.

Laurie would finish the books. Of course! He was capable, a neat worker – but more important, he was interested in them. He loved the old books quite possibly as much as his employer. And as she sat down at the table, now cleared of the old papers, Vanessa began to plan how she would persuade Laurie to carry on where she left off. He was coming again on Monday. He clearly had every intention of working with her each morning, and it seemed to be accepted by everyone. A satisfactory arrangement, a painless transfer. The books would be done, that was what mattered.

Vanessa began to feel a little better as she began eating. Just a little, but it was enough for now.

It came back to her later that day as she went down to the gymnasium. Cal had not been at lunch, but Andrew Maclean had, and had set out to be particularly charming to Vanessa, as indeed he had been all morning. He had told her something of his business commitments, and despite everything she had felt a growing admiration for him. He was clearly dedicated to his work, had interests in companies scattered as far afield as Aberdeen and London, and obviously derived satisfaction from travelling around Britain and Europe. And underneath, too, she was made aware of a certain sensitivity in his manner. Yet her father had told her that *his* father was ruthless. Yet again, the picture did not tie up. In a complete state of turmoil she went into the gymnasium, hoping against hope that Cal Grayne would not have changed into his *judoka*, and that she would somehow be able to persuade him not to bother. His eyes were too shrewd, too clear-seeing. She did not know what he would see in hers. She didn't want to find out.

The gymnasium was silent, and Vanessa walked across it towards the changing rooms, then called out: 'Cal?' Immediately she realized she had used his first name, and bit her lip. Yet there was no choice. She was even more reluctant to call him Mr. Grayne, for fear of his ever-ready laughter – at her.

'I'll not be a moment.' So he was there after all. He came out of the changing room a second later, and looked questioningly at her. Vanessa knew that traces of the morning's upset remained in her face, the delicate shadows of fatigue that make-up could not erase or hide, and she took a deep breath, not wanting him to see, yet not able to do anything about it.

'I just wondered if you were here,' she said. 'I couldn't hear any movement.'

He was looking at her now as if puzzled, and she wondered in fleeting alarm if her grandfather had told him about the scene in her room. She hoped not – but nothing was sure.

'I'm here all right,' he answered. 'Are you ready?'

She hesitated, but only for a moment. 'Yes. It won't take me long to change. Excuse me.' She moved past him, he stood aside, and she went into the changing room and closed the door. What to do now? She really had no choice. She must go through with it, even though she felt weak.

Several minutes later they were facing each other across the *tatami* mat, the same spot as the previous day. Gradually she relaxed as they loosened up, for he was impersonal again, as before, which made it easier for Vanessa.

He made her practise a few of the previous day's falls for several minutes. She was surprised at how quickly it all came back to her, and in fact Cal commented on it a short while later, during a pause for breath.

'You're a natural, you know,' he said.

She looked quickly at him, suspecting sarcasm, and he smiled. 'No, I mean it. You're very supple and slim.'

'Thank you,' she chanced a smile at him. Knowing that she would so soon be leaving lessened her fear of him slightly. The innuendoes, the veiled questions, none of them would matter in another week or so.

Suddenly he asked: 'Aren't you well?'

'Why, I – yes.' She frowned. 'W-why do you ask?'

'You look very pale – you mustn't carry on if you don't feel up to it.' Then very swiftly, quite out of the blue: 'Did Laurie upset you?'

Vanessa jerked her head up at that. For a moment she genuinely could not think what he meant. 'Laurie? I don't understand.'

'You went out to meet him this morning – you were upset when you came back.'

Light dawned. She shook her head. 'Oh no,' she breathed. 'It wasn't him. It was—' and she stopped, and looked at him. 'Please,' she said. 'I don't want to talk about it.' Without realizing it, she had backed slightly away from him, but Cal saw, and his eyes narrowed.

'Don't tell me I frighten you?' he asked harshly.

'No – only when you—' She stopped again, and the awful trapped feeling was there, rising in her breast, stifling her. 'No,' she said. 'Please, let's get on with the lesson,' and she shook her head in soft despair, so that her hair swung round against her cheeks, silkily caressing the pale skin.

'I can't teach you in this state,' he said. 'Not when you're so obviously terrified of me—'

'I'm not!' she burst out. 'Not when you're teaching me. You're fine. But when you start asking me – I – I don't want to—' Her voice tailed away. It was no use. He wouldn't let her go now – not until she had told him everything – until he had forced the truth from her. Never that. *Never*. Eyes wide, she stared at him, then as he moved slightly, panicked. She just turned and ran away, across the mat, and into the changing room. But before she could shut the door he was there, his arm outthrust, pushing it wide open.

'For God's sake, girl,' he said. 'What *is* it?'

'Go away. I want you to go away,' she whispered. 'Please.'

'Not until I know why you're so terrified. I can't leave you like this—'

'Yes. I don't want to talk to you. Go away!' She did something very foolish in her despair. She tried to push him away from her. She might as well have tried pushing at a solid wall. He didn't budge an inch, but he did put his arms up to hold hers.

'No. Now tell me what's the matter. You've been crying your eyes out, haven't you?'

Vanessa didn't answer. She stared at him, then with the hard directness of his gaze on her, looked away, sideways. It was better when she didn't face him, and he couldn't hold her for ever. She didn't *have* to speak. He couldn't force her, could he? But the tension was there, building up again quickly because of their very nearness in that tiny room, even though the door was open. And she tried to pull herself free.

'Haven't you?' he demanded. 'Tell me.'

'Yes, *yes*, all right, I have.' She swung back to face him. 'Now what are you going to do about it? What is it to do with you anyway? *Nothing*. You're too damned nosey. Now leave me alone, let me go! You can't hold me against my will – I *hate* you!'

'No, you don't. You don't hate me. And I'm so damned nosey because your crying is tied up with the reason you're here, isn't it?'

How could he have guessed that? Her gasp of dismay could not be hidden, because he was too near the truth – *far* too near, and any minute ... Fear gave her the strength to pull her arms free from his grasp, to turn away, pick up her shoes and turn back. 'I'm going to change. *Right now*,' she said. 'Do you hear me?'

'What's your real name?' he asked softly.

'Vanessa Collins. I've already told you.' The answer was quick, but not quick enough.

'And Smith. Yes, I remember. You told me. But I don't believe you.'

'Then go to hell! I don't care what you believe! You're a bully. I don't want you to teach me anything! You hear me? I *hate* bullies.'

There was a sudden electric silence that lasted for several seconds, the two of them just standing there, watching each other, then Cal turned round and went out, and shut the door behind him. Vanessa sat down on the wooden stool in the corner, her legs too weak to support her any longer. He had not given up, that was clear. The sooner she left Deanston House, the better. Because one way or another, Cal would discover her secret if she stayed much longer.

CHAPTER SEVEN

THE knowledge she carried inside her would grow heavier every day, she knew that now. It was there when she went into the library the following morning to begin her day's work, the sense of oppression, the thought that perhaps this was where the signatures had been written, hour after hour, and on one occasion thrust quickly among a pile of old newspapers because someone had entered – and then been forgotten ... A memory of something her grandfather had said and done strengthened that theory. Vanessa stood quite still as she recalled his face, the lost look when the papers had been mentioned. Perhaps he was thinking back to a mutual interest, shared with his son – and soon shattered.

She donned a clean blue overall and began to set out a pile of books to be gone through and listed. Her heart was heavy. Now she had a task with Laurie, something to find out as soon as possible.

Her opportunity came as they drank their morning coffee at eleven. He put a particularly old book to one side with care, patted it gently, and sighed.

'You really love those books, don't you?' Vanessa asked.

He looked at her, an expression of amusement coming slowly. 'I suppose so – if I'd ever thought about it. Why do you ask?'

'Well, I just wonder why you didn't offer to catalogue them when you knew Mr. Maclean was looking for somebody.'

'Me?' he shook his head. 'Och, I never thought of it – besides, my job's doing the gardens. This is not man's work.' Vanessa repressed the slight smile that threatened at the touch of scorn in his voice. She had to be careful now.

'Of course it is!' she answered quickly. 'Heavens, it requires intelligence and a good brain – and care. A lot of men do this sort of work. And you're so good at it.'

'Am I?' he seemed to be considering that. 'I was only doing it to help you – I never thought—'

'I couldn't manage without you.' And it was true. She knew it as she said it. She had to be *very* careful now. 'Only, Laurie, if I – if I couldn't finish it for any reason – would you?'

He put his cup and saucer carefully down on the table. His eyes were very bright on her – very shrewd. 'All right, out wi' it,' he said.

'Why, there's nothing—' she began.

'Ach, come off it!' He had never spoken to her like that before, and it came as a shock. 'I bet it's that damned Cal Grayne! What's he done now, eh?'

She went weak with relief. So that was what he thought. It would be almost funny at another time. First Cal assuming Laurie had upset her, now this!

'Oh, Laurie! No, it's nothing like *that*. I—'

'Listen. You were near to tears yesterday morning. I'm not daft, you know.'

'I never thought you were.' She put out her hand to touch his arm. 'I'd had some bad news about – about a relative – and I was rather upset. It had nothing to do with *him*, I promise you. It's just – I'm not sure if I can stay here much longer, that's all. And I don't want to leave my – Mr. Maclean—' she had nearly slipped up

143

then, nearly said 'my grandfather', '—in the lurch, that's all.'

Laurie looked down at her hand resting on his arm, and covered it with his own.

'I'd have a job to refuse you anything, wouldn't I?' he said softly. 'But I don't want you to leave, you know that fine well.' He gave her a wry grin. 'So if I refuse to help, will you stay?'

She shook her head. 'I can't. Perhaps another week or so, but that's all. Please, please, Laurie, what I've just told you is in strict confidence. I can trust you, can't I? You won't say anything?'

'I won't say anything to anybody, I promise,' he assured her. 'But I may try and talk *you* out of it.'

She smiled at him. 'Thanks. I feel a lot better now, really. Look – hadn't you better have your coffee before it gets cold?' But as she turned away to pick up her own drink, the smile left her face. She should never have come, she knew that now. So much deception, so many lies to be told. Mr. Murton had been right, only in a way he couldn't have imagined. She would have done better to listen to him after all.

The next two days passed slowly. Vanessa worked hard, trying to do as much as she could before the inevitable day dawned when she would tell her grandfather she was leaving. Every meal with him was a torment, not helped by Cal Grayne, who treated her with a cool politeness that was almost intimidating. It was as if he watched her, waiting for her to make a wrong move, and her nerves gradually stretched to breaking point. On Wednesday afternoon she was alone in the library when Cal came in. Instantly she was tense, on her guard, waiting for something – she knew not what – that might mean he was after her again.

But he seemed casual enough. 'I'm sorry to interrupt you,' he said. 'I've just come for a book,' and he walked down to the end where the modern books were kept, the part that had no concern with Vanessa's work. She watched him, waiting for him to leave so that she could get on with her writing. He reached down, riffled along several books, then pulled one out. She almost heard his soft sigh of satisfaction from where she was standing. Then he turned back and looked at her. 'You must tell me,' he said, in a very polite casual tone, 'when you want the newspapers bringing down again. That is, if you've been through them.' She tried to hide the shock his words had given her. Since finding the incriminating papers she had been most reluctant to even touch any of the others, and had carefully put them back in the box, in a corner of her bedroom, and covered them with some women's magazines.

'I – I haven't been through them yet. I haven't had time.' Her heart was beating rapidly, bumping against her ribs so that it nearly hurt her. Had he done it deliberately? Did he guess anything? 'They can come down any time you like. They – they'll have to be done l-later. I'm too busy on these now.' She waved her arm to the stack of books behind her on the table.

'Hmm,' he nodded, and turned away. 'I'll go and fetch them now.' Then he paused just as he was about to go out. 'Oh, I'm sorry. You are coming, aren't you?'

'Yes.' Vanessa put the card down that she had been clutching in her hand and went towards the door. She bit her lip. In every word he said she sensed deliberate taunts, felt the hard suspicion – and dislike too? He opened the door wide for her to pass him, then walked beside her to the stairs. Her heart was still hammering, but now it wasn't with fear, it was at his nearness, and the tingling awareness that filled her because they were walking beside each other up the stairs, to the top, along the landing, still in silence that she dared not break for fear she would invite his scorn with whatever words she spoke.

Then they were at her door. Cal waited for her to open it, and she went in. 'In a box by the window. I put some magazines on top – just a moment.' She went to lift them off, waited for him, watched him pick up the heavy box with ease. The hard green eyes met hers, and he said softly:

'Are they all here?'

'Yes. Every one.' Except, she realized suddenly, the two pages that had caused her such anguish. She closed her eyes for a second in pain. Better if she had never seen them. She opened her eyes, and he was watching her. And it was as if he knew. A sudden sharp pain stabbed her as she fought for breath. She could not bear it any longer. If she didn't get away from this man she would go mad. She turned quickly away, to go to the door, uncaring whether he followed or not, unable to stay in the same room with him any longer. She closed the door very quietly after he had gone, giving him time to cross the landing before she followed. She went very slowly after him, not making it appear too deliberate, but making sure she didn't have to walk down beside him.

He reached the library well ahead of her, and went in, and she dawdled across the hall . . .

'I've put the box back where it was before.'

'Yes, thank you.' She went in and closed the door. The gap left in the line of books caught her eyes, and she crossed to the shelves, taking a quick look back to make sure he wasn't going to come in again ... The missing book was from the middle of a series of several with similar jackets. She picked up the immediate neighbour, and recognized a travel book that she had read. Cal was writing a book about a journey – that vague thought crossed her mind. Perhaps he needed to refer to something.

The author was Callum Kyle. She pulled a face at the name, the same as Cal's, and opened the back cover page to see the almost inevitable picture of the author, a darkly bearded man who could have been any age ... Then she looked closer, disbelief followed by astonishment, followed by realization, as she recognized the man behind the beard. It was Cal.

So Cal Grayne was Callum Kyle, well-known writer, traveller, and broadcaster. She had to look at him across the dinner table and wondered why she hadn't realized that fact before. She had read and enjoyed two of his books, for he had the rare gift of immediacy in his writing, so that for those few hours of reading you really were *there*, with him, in the desert, or among mountain peasants, eating their local dishes, tasting them. She would not have imagined it. This man, Callum Kyle. Ironic that he should accuse her of using a false name when he had one himself. There was a difference, of course; his was a pseudonym for writing purposes. Perhaps that was why he was sensitive to others' names too. Vanessa bent to her sweet, and wondered if she would manage to escape. She felt stifled in the house. It was a fine clear evening, and she thought that a walk might do her good – clear her head too.

As they left the dining-room she asked her grandfather, 'I'd like to go for a walk – perhaps down to the gate. Do you mind?'

'Mind? Of course not. Go where you wish.'

'Thanks. I need some exercise, and it's a pleasant evening. I'll just go and get a cardigan.' She turned and left them, and did not see the look her grandfather gave to Cal.

She set off walking, breathing in the scented evening air, glad she had brought her cardigan, for there was a nip in the air, a promise of mist and dampness later. Parts of the drive were shadowy with tree branches overhanging, and the huge rhododendrons, but she wasn't bothered. After all that had happened recently she felt that nothing worse could overtake her. She was drained of energy, the nervous strain already beginning to tell on her, her appetite nearly vanished altogether, so that even Mrs. Banks' delicious cooking had ceased to appeal.

And now, alone, away from the house, she had time to think. Inside, the subtle pressures were too strong to let her concentrate, the presence of Cal, and above all her grandfather, who, she was beginning to realize, was not the cruel unkind man her father had made out. Of course he had a streak of hardness, she had seen that occasionally, but she had also seen the way he was most of the time, kind, considerate, *caring*. He had cared on Sunday morning sufficiently to stay at home with an employee and talk to her, tell her amusing anecdotes of a busy life with much travelling and meeting people in it. That, in a way, had done it, that and the admittance at last to herself of something she had known subconsciously for years but had managed to deny until now.

Her father had been weak and foolish – and now, it seemed, dishonest as well. She stopped, near the gate, and looked beyond it to the road stretching away, a grey ribbon cutting through bleak hills. Snow gleamed on top of one, blue-misted, far away. Vanessa lifted her eyes to it, not really seeing it, so engrossed in her own thoughts was she, and came to her decision. She must not just run away. Before she went, she would write her grandfather a letter and tell him of the cruel deceit she had practised, simply out of a mistaken idea of revenge. That much she owed to him. Then she would leave. She would end her letter by asking for forgiveness – without much hope of receiving it, for was she not her father's daughter? And he had let this father down too. Andrew Maclean would not want a granddaughter tainted the same way.

She blinked back treacherous tears. No more crying. She had done enough of that. And Cal Grayne would be satisfied to be found right. Or would he? Despite everything, Vanessa wondered. He seemed fond of her grandfather – and if he married Heather, and Andrew Maclean married Anne Macrae, they would be related. Vanessa reached out to touch the gatepost, a bleak lonely feeling filling her as the scene in the dining-room came irresistibly back. The four of them, talking, laughing, drinking together, and she the intruder. She turned away from the gate. Perhaps Heather would have the judo lessons now. Vanessa could not imagine her allowing her hair to be ruffled in the slightest. And how would she like the outfit she would have to wear, the *judoka*?

As she walked slowly back up the drive, Vanessa's lip trembled in what was nearly a smile. That could be funny – only she would not be there to see it. And the smile vanished.

She quickened her steps. Now that the decision was made about the letter, she knew she would have to write it soon.

Lights were on in the rooms, and as she neared it, she stopped, an ache tugging at her heart at the sight of the gracious old house that stood there, aloof and dignified. No wonder Cal came here to write. What better surroundings for a writer to work? And no wonder her grandfather came home each time from his travels with, as he had told Vanessa on Sunday, a great feeling of relief and happiness. She knew exactly what he meant now, looking at it, sensing the atmosphere that pervaded the very stones. She bit her lip. Fate could play cruel tricks at times. It had allowed her to glimpse what might have been, and soon she must go away for ever, because that was the way it had to be. She began walking again, ran up the steps and pushed open the front door. The heavy ticking of the clock greeted her, and the sound of men's voices from the lounge, faintly. They were laughing at something.

Vanessa went quickly and quietly up the stairs, and into her room. She took out her notepad and envelopes and put them on the bedside table.

Laurie came on Thursday as usual, soon after nine in the morning. He looked at Vanessa as he came in, then grinned. 'Changed your mind yet?'

She shook her head. 'No, I'm sorry, Laurie. Would you like to do some of the listing this morning, instead of me?'

He pulled a face. 'I see. Getting me trained?'

'I'm sorry, I didn't mean it to sound like that. Oh, Laurie, I'm so mixed up!' She put her hand to her cheek, and he came over to her.

'Don't, Vanessa. Don't be upset. Och, can't I do *anything* to help?'

'No, there's nothing.' She thought of the letter hidden safely in a dressing table drawer upstairs, written and sealed, waiting only to be delivered when the time came.

Laurie tilted her chin up, a gesture oddly reminiscent of Cal, yet different. 'You're not going to cry, are you?'

His face was so worried that she had to smile. 'Oh no!' She didn't think she could even if she wanted to.

'Thank goodness!' He sounded greatly relieved, ran his free hand through his thick hair. 'Look, will I get you a cup of tea or coffee?'

'Heavens! Mrs. Banks would probably give in her notice!'

'I know. But I'm prepared to try and shock her if you want one.'

'No, really. I only had breakfast a short while ago.' And *that* had been an awful meal with Cal and herself alone, he cool and formal – and watching her as if puzzled, and she unable to eat more than a small piece of toast. Even that had been an effort, and she knew that if he had so much as asked her if anything was wrong, she would have got up and walked out. But he hadn't. Perhaps he had sensed her mood, seen the tautness that now filled her, from which she could not escape – and would not until she walked out of the house and drove away.

'Well, if you're sure. Tell me if you want one. For you I'll brave the lion – I mean, lioness!'

'Thanks, Laurie. You're kind, really.'

He turned away abruptly. 'Well, we'd better get started, hadn't we? What are you going to do?'

'I'll put these other books back in order.' She pointed at a pile neatly stacked by the window, listed and indexed, ready to go back on the shelves. Already the work they were doing was having results. It was satisfying in a way to see the books going back all listed and numbered, knowing that in a few weeks all would be done – only I won't be here to see it, she thought, with a sudden pang. Laurie will, but I'll have gone. She went quickly to begin her task, as if to chase the treacherous thoughts away. In that way the morning passed quickly. There was one bright spot she had to look forward to. Neither Cal nor her grandfather would be in to dinner that evening, and she was going to have hers in her room, an arrangement which, at the moment, suited her only too well. If only she could have all her meals there. Although Mrs. Banks would doubtless have something to say about that, she thought wryly as she carried six books to the shelves. She put them on in neat order, turned to watch Laurie as he bent to his task, and felt a slight lift of spirit. There was no difficulty there, she knew that now. He had taken to the job so quickly and easily. If only her grandfather had known before, he would have asked him to do the work, she felt sure.

The afternoon was quiet without Laurie, but Vanessa was used to this now, and when she finished work at five and took a last look round the library before leaving, she wondered how he would get on with Cal when *he* was working alone. Perhaps they would both have the sense to leave each other strictly alone. She saw the gap left by the removal of his book from the far shelves, and walked across and picked another of his books out to look through later. She had plenty to read, but the urge to read a book of his, in the light of knowledge, of actually knowing its author, was quite strong. She went out, closing the door quietly behind her, and ran upstairs. Cal's bedroom was at the far side of the house, at the other end of the long wide landing to her own. Faintly from it Vanessa heard the rhythmic tap-tap of a typewriter, as she so often did. She walked quickly into her room and closed the door.

She heard the men leave the house about six, while the news was on television. She went quietly to the window and watched her grandfather climb into Cal's waiting Jaguar, its engine note a muted roar as he leaned over to open the door. It went off down the drive and she watched it go. Another hour and Mrs. Banks would bring her dinner on a tray. A simpler meal than usual, with the men not there, but that suited Vanessa. Her appetite had dwindled to nothing in the last few days, and even the thought of Mrs. Banks' truly delicious meals held no attraction for her. She leaned against the window ledge, sunk in a misery that she thought would never pass. Mr. Murton's disapproving face swam into view, mistily, and she imagined going in to tell him what had happened. She owed him that at least. Then she would move away from her flat, move out of London – maybe go abroad to work, for she felt restless, as she never had before in her life. The window pane was cool to her forehead. For a moment she wondered if she was about to get a cold, or influenza. Her whole body ached, her face felt as if it were on fire, yet a wave of coldness swept through her as she stood there.

Vanessa moved away from the window. Cal's book lay on the table. She picked it up, turned off the television, and went to sit in the large easy chair. It was strange, reading the opening words, the explanation of how he had converted a Land-Rover into a virtual home on wheels for a trip through a remote area of Africa. Strange because this was not just another book from a library shelf. Each word was written by a man who had saved her from a pair of young thugs; a man who suspected and disliked her. In mid-sentence Vanessa stopped reading and flicked through the pages to the photograph on the back again. How different he looked with a beard! She didn't like them particularly, but his suited him. And he lived here, in the same house, and in a few days she would be leaving it for good — and how that would please him. The eyes in the photograph were watching her, mocking, cynical — mysterious. She took a deep breath and turned the pages back to the one she was reading. She made a determined effort — she must do, but the image of the writer kept coming between her and the black print. He had held her, kissed her, taken hold of her to show her how to fall ... and been quite gentle for a change ... Vanessa's breath caught in her throat, and warmth filled her at the memory of those strong arms, his eyes — his eyes.

She flung the book down beside her and stood up to go to the window. Without thinking, she put her fingers to her mouth and touched her lips. He had kissed her — the first man to do so without seeming to *care* one way or another whether he actually did or not. The gardens stretched out beautifully before her, unrolling in all their splendour into the distance, and in the furthest reaches she could see the hills, grey and rugged with the everlasting snow clearly visible, deep patches that would never melt, because on those bleak summits it was never warm enough.

There was a knock at the door and she turned to greet Mrs. Banks, relieved at the interruption to thoughts that threatened to become disturbing. The evening seemed to stretch ahead endlessly after she had finished eating. She took the tray downstairs to save the housekeeper having to come up for it. There was a comedy on television, and she watched that until the news came on at ten. She felt restless and unhappy and knew that she would not sleep. Outside everything was still and quiet, the light soft with night fast approaching, cool and misty, the ideal time for a walk to clear her head – and perhaps to tire her.

Vanessa found a thick cardigan and put it on, switched off television and went downstairs. Outside the air was tangy and cool and beautiful. She began to walk round the back of the house, past the place where she had met Laurie, and along the path which gradually grew more shadowy. She estimated that she would eventually come to the garages, although the usual way was round the other side of the house. A minute later she saw them, a series of outbuildings that had at one time been stables. A light showed from the kitchen overlooking them, and a huge lamp attached to the garage roof acted as a floodlight, casting bright yellow for many yards in either direction. She stopped for a moment to look. The garage doors were rarely closed, save in bad weather, and her car stood there, a blank space beside it showing where Cal's Jaguar had been parked. She wondered if the two men would be very late in. Not that it mattered, how could it? But Heather's beautiful golden face swam into view, her smile sweet upon her lips. The smile she had for Cal.

Vanessa began to walk on quickly, determined to find out before she left exactly where the drive did lead to. She went on, and all the time the path curved gently round, and the trees cast their eerie shadows, and the sky darkened in that way it has in Scotland; the gravel was crunchy underfoot, the only noise – apart from the occasional crackle from the undergrowth as a bird was startled at her passing.

And then Vanessa came upon the lake, and stopped in astonishment. It was small, with a little island in the middle, and a bridge leading to it, and rocks fashioned into an artificial cave. A vague memory stirred at the back of her mind, something her father had once said about a place he had played in childhood. This must be it. A lake with an island; a veritable paradise for an imaginative boy. Something caught in her throat at that thought – a sad reminder of everything that had come to pass since.

She walked nearer and felt the wooden handrail of the bridge. It was old and needed painting, but seemed strong enough. She tested the planks with her foot. They creaked slightly, and from somewhere in the distance an owl hooted, an eerie ghostly sound. She let her hand fall, and turned away. She wouldn't try and walk to the island, not tonight, perhaps tomorrow. But even as the thought came she knew she would not. Not ever now.

Further round there was a bench, almost hidden in the shadows. Vanessa went and sat on it, watching the graceful weeping willows trailing their delicate fronds in the still waters of the lake. Memories rushed back strongly; memories of her father as he had been when she was younger, carefree, always laughing – or seemingly so in memory. But the mind could play tricks, so that the days we wanted to remember always seemed as if made of gold. Later there had come the bitterness; the bitterness that had made Vanessa come all this way seeking revenge.

She stared at the water with unseeing eyes. The journey was nearly over, the mission failed. And she looked ahead to the days which lay in front of her, the long dark days in London, alone in her flat. Alone. There were friends of both sexes, always would be, but she knew in a sudden flash of illumination that that was not enough. She needed someone to lean on; she was tired of being independent. Loneliness was in her eyes and face as she looked down to the darkening ground before her. It was growing cooler now, faint stars beginning to show in a darkened sky. A bird darted past high overhead, a black blur against the paler background. Vanessa had never felt so lost and lonely in all her life. With a soft cry of despair she leaned forward and covered her face with her hands.

It was there that Cal Grayne found her several minutes later. She didn't see him. She saw nothing, for her eyes were closed behind those sheltering hands as she sat very still on the bench, seeing her grandfather's expression as it had been when he had come upon her weeping in her bedroom. Her shoulders drooped, her slender arms seemed too fragile to support the weight of her sadness, and Cal Grayne stood where he was in the shadows for a few long moments just watching her, but his face gave nothing of his feelings away. It was as inscrutable as a mask.

Then he went quietly forward and touched her on the shoulder.

'Vanessa?'

Startled, she looked up. 'Go away.' The words came out without any conscious thought. She didn't want him; she didn't want anybody at that moment. But he sat beside her and she turned her head quickly away.

'No, it's late, and it's dark, and you'll be getting lost.' Lost! That was funny! If only he knew how lost she was already!

'I won't. I can find my way back. Leave me alone – please.' She turned to look at him, not caring what he might see in her face now. Nothing seemed to matter any more. Just getting away . . .

'Come on. It's getting cold. You're shivering.' It was true. Strange she had not noticed it. She ran her hands up her arms, feeling the goose pimples there. Then she heard the rustle of cloth, and the next moment something warm and heavy came over her shoulders. Startled, she turned to see him jacketless, lifted her hand to touch the suede, and began: 'But you—'

'Yes. And I can't sit out here all night in my shirt-sleeves, can I? So are you coming?' Vanessa found herself on her feet, not sure whether he had helped her, or whether she had accomplished it herself. They began walking, and the coat was very warm and had that faintly elusive tang of good cigars about it. Vanessa had put her arms up to make sure it didn't slip off, hands crossed, holding the front together.

'Thank you for lending me your jacket,' she said after a few moments walking in a not uncomfortable silence.

She looked at him walking beside her, his shirt gleaming faintly white in the dusk, his shoulders broad and powerful. 'But are you sure—'

'I never feel the cold,' he answered, reached out and touched her hand with his own. 'Feel that.' His hand was warm. The touch was brief and impersonal, lasting a mere few seconds, but she felt the warmth after he had taken it away, and a treacherous tingle that spread and filled her with sudden fire.

To cover up the faint confusion that followed, she said quickly: 'I didn't think you'd be back so early.'

'No. We're not usually, but Mrs. Macrae wasn't too well, so—' he shrugged. Vanessa couldn't help the quick thought: Heather wouldn't like that! The idea was strangely pleasing.

'Your light wasn't on, and Mrs. Banks said she'd heard you go out ages ago—' Had she really been out that long? It seemed no time at all since ... 'So I said I'd go and see if you'd gone for a ride, you hadn't, obviously, so I decided to walk round here and see – and there you were.'

There was something the matter with him. He wasn't his normal self, but Vanessa could not tell what the difference was. She sensed the change, but it wasn't until later on, when she was in bed, that she was able to pinpoint it.

An hour later she was in her own room, sitting in bed with a cup of steaming cocoa in her hands. She thought back to that return walk from the lake, for now there was time to think properly for the first time. There had been none before. Her grandfather had been waiting in the hall, the expression on his face one of anxiety, but his tone relieved as he said:

'There you are! My dear, come in, come in,' and he had taken her arm and ushered her into the lounge. In a way it had been like a nightmare, for his behaviour only underlined her thoughts so much more strongly, emphasizing the sharp bitterness, the anguish newly felt . . .

She had managed to escape, after a while, handing the coat back to the watchful Cal, saying she was tired. would they excuse her? They would – but Cal's expression remained with her as she ran upstairs – and came back to her now as she sipped the sweet cocoa that Mrs. Banks had made.

She knew what the change was; knew what was wrong. He was behaving completely differently to her – even *looking* differently at her, not in that cool slightly calculating way that always made her feel uneasy, but in another manner. More like a man who has made a discovery. But of what? The question teased Vanessa as she sat in bed, the sheets tucked in round her deliciously warm, for the night had gone quite cool. Then realization came, and with it disbelief. He *knew*. He knew who she was. She put the cup down in the saucer standing on her bedside table, fearful that she would spill the drink if she continued to hold it. She felt her forehead, pressing hard as if that might help her to think more clearly. 'Oh, my God!' she whispered the three words, unaware of saying them out loud. He knew. She didn't know how he had found out, but the growing certainty was within her. And now she knew she must leave very soon, must go away from Deanston House for ever.

CHAPTER EIGHT

VANESSA was composed the next morning, calm and cool as she went into breakfast. If Cal was going to say anything, he would have done so the previous night, outside, when she had so clearly been so vulnerable to attack. But he had not. Did that mean he was saving it for some other time? Vanessa didn't know, she only knew that she could no longer stay here. On the following day, Saturday, she would leave. And before she went, she would put out the letter for Mrs. Banks to find.

She watched Laurie very attentively that morning. It was as if it were important that he be able to do all the work properly before she left. And she wasn't going to tell him. When they said good-bye at lunch, it would be for the last time, only he wouldn't know that. He was cheerful, his usual self, as if determined not to mention anything about leaving to her. They had coffee at eleven, and Laurie was enjoying the work, for he spoke of the books as if he personally had discovered them, amusing Vanessa slightly, for it was ironic in a way that this should happen now, now that her decision was made, and irrevocably. It was also heartening. At least there would be no guilty pangs about the books to add to all her other burdens.

At one he looked at the clock and smiled, stretching as he stood up. 'Ach well, I'm off to do some gardening this afternoon,' he said. 'I like this life. Books in the morning – and you. The gardens afterwards.'

Vanessa smiled. 'I'm glad. I'm only surprised that you didn't find out about this work before, and offer, you do it so well – better than me.'

He shook his head. 'Ach, I'd never have even started on it, if it hadn't been for you coming down the path that morning.'

She smiled. 'Thanks anyway, Laurie. Good-bye.' She wanted to add, and thank you for helping, but he would have been suspicious, so she said it silently as he went out of the door.

'I'll see you on Monday,' he said, but the door shutting behind him hid her whispered: 'No, you won't.'

She looked round, waited a moment to give him time to leave, then went out herself.

Cal was alone in the dining-room. Vanessa took a deep breath and walked to her place. 'Don't get up, please,' she said as he made as if to stand. She looked at him coolly as she sat down. Since the meeting by the lake the previous night something had changed between them. Most odd really, for she expected to feel frightened of him – of the undoubted power he now possessed if her guess was right. But she didn't. And she did not understand why. Perhaps, she thought, as she began her soup, it was because she would so soon be away – and she would never see him again. Her hand stopped, full of soup, half way to her mouth. She would never see him again. Never. And she looked up and thought: What a funny time to discover that you're in love with a man you thought you hated!

She put the spoon down carefully in her plate, and Cal looked up from his own and said: 'What's the matter? Soup no good?'

'No. No – I just—' and how awful if she said the

truth: 'I just realized that I don't dislike you at all. In fact I think I love you.' She could imagine the unrestrained laughter at that. 'I don't want any more,' she finished, and he frowned slightly.

'But you're not eating at all lately. Are you ill?'

'No, of course not.' Leave me alone, she prayed. Please leave me alone. She knew every inch of his face, had done ever since that first time she had met him – when he had strode across and demanded to know her name, and now she knew *why*. She couldn't help it. She had to look at him again, to see the dark features filled it seemed, with concern. Cal – concerned? Difficult to believe. She couldn't stay.

She stood up. 'I think I'll go to my room. Will you excuse me? And explain to m – Mr. Maclean—' She had nearly given herself away then. She would have to watch that in the few hours remaining for her at the house. 'Please tell him I don't feel very well—' She was walking away from the table now, and Cal didn't try to stop her. He didn't say anything, just remained where he was. Vanessa went out of the room. She was thankful he had made no move. She would have started crying if he had.

She waited in her room until she heard her grandfather go into the dining-room, then she slipped quietly down the stairs and out of the front door. She wasn't clear where she was going, only that she needed to get away from the house for a little while. She ran along the path to the back of the house – and saw the garage, the doors invitingly open, her car standing there.

Vanessa felt in her bag for her keys, found them, and ran across to the shadowy building that had once held horses. The engine rumbled and grumbled, then started, and she backed out, very careful not to touch the shiny Jaguar beside hers. She needed a ride to clear her head, and she knew where she would go. High in the hills the road wound up, and eventually dwindled into what had probably once been a small community. Now just a few roofless shells of houses remained, and sheep rubbed their backs against three-foot-thick walls, and sheltered from the sharp winds there. The place was quiet, a little ghostly perhaps, but not in an unfriendly way.

She drove along to the gates, saw Laurie wave in the distance, his dog by his side, and gave him a brief answering wave. Perhaps it would be only fair to write him a note as well. Yes, she could do that...

The road curved nicely upwards, and the evening was cool and fresh, and she wound down her window to let the wind blow her hair about her face. Now was the time to look around, to store the memories for that future that awaited her. The road was narrow, with passing places whose signs were rusty. No one ever came this way now, and the hills towered bleakly to the right. To the left, distantly, water gleamed, and gulls flew high overhead crying sadly. A beautiful melancholy spot, and apparently forgotten by the rest of the world. Vanessa wondered briefly what it must have been like to live there, so remote from anywhere, with just the trees and bushes for company; and the towering snow-topped hills standing in their aloof majesty, strong, immovable, older than time.

She drove off the bumpy track and along a field for several yards, then switched off. Silence fell as the engine died, and she turned on the radio for a few minutes before she went for a walk. For she had a certain shocking discovery to think about on that walk, and she wanted to postpone the moment. Perhaps even the music was in conspiracy with Cal. The mellow tones of an improbably named singer, Clint Gravel, floated from the dashboard radio with his latest disc, a catchy, heart-tugging little tune – and the words he sang were so appropriate and painful that Vanessa reached out to switch off again, but hesitated for a moment as the words came out:

'—but why do I love you? I wish that I could run away, because you are so cruel . . .' Click. It was off. She got out and slammed the door shut behind her. Coincidence, that was all. 'But why do I love you?' she whispered the words aloud, and a sheep lumbered to its feet, startled at this intrusion, first of a car, now a human.

Cal's face came into her mind; she was helpless to resist it, the image of him as she had seen him first, in the café, when he had looked up briefly from his paper and away again, a short sharp dismissive glance. Then in action as she had watched him effortlessly stun the two youths. And later, temper flaring on the landing when they had argued briefly and sharply. Gentle with a kiss, cruel with those probing questions . . . and just now, so recently at dinner, with concern on his face. But the one incident above all these had been on the previous night, at that moment she had felt his jacket slipping warmly over her shoulders. That little walk home had been different – and she had known why afterwards. Somehow he knew. Vanessa took a deep breath and went to sit on a low tumbledown wall, watching a young sheep eyeing her with mistrust. She reached out a hand. 'Come on,' she whispered, coaxing, and it turned and skittered away in alarm, making her smile.

Everywhere was silent. Only very distantly the mew of gulls, no other noises, no cars or people to disturb the silence of a warm summer evening that had been a momentous one for Vanessa. For she had never imagined herself in love before, had never looked at a man and known the sharp sweet pain that can come with the realization of love.

'Oh, God, what a fool I've been.' She said the words aloud in her anguish, because there was no one to hear them. She had wondered, on the journey here from London, at the very beginning, if she had made a big mistake. And now she had the answer. She had. For in meeting her grandfather, and getting to know him – even if only slightly – she had gained a more complete picture than that given her by her father. Vanessa looked over to the nearest house, because a fat lamb had wandered out, bleating for its mother. But she didn't really see the animal, she was back again in that room with her father, the man she loved so dearly – but was now realizing had faults and frailties like any other human being – maybe more than some. That was what had hurt – the knowledge that her beloved father was less than perfect. She must destroy the two papers before she left. That at least she owed to them both – father and grandfather. Then a new life to build out of the ruins of old bitterness. Time would heal the deepest wounds, and she would find that Deanston House, and the people who lived there could be thought of without pain. Perhaps . . .

Vanessa stood up and began to walk. A good long ramble was what she needed, some exercise and less introspection. She strode out, long-legged, slim and graceful, dark hair swinging free, and she found pleasure in the movement, the springy ground underfoot that was peaty and heathery. The track had petered out, trees and rocks were her companions, with occasional sheep watchful, yellow-eyed, suspicious. She was climbing gradually, and saw a spring tumble down from the rocks, the water diamond-bright and sparkling in the evening sun, and watched it for a few moments, leaning down to run her hand in the icy freshness, then dabbing her face. It tasted of peat and heather, and she cupped her hands and drank some before moving on again.

Trees grew thicker now and soon there was a forest of pines, tall and straight and mysterious, and no one to see it all, save her.

She walked in among the trees, and the air went suddenly colder, almost chill, so that she shivered, but she went on in, for there was something soothing in the very atmosphere, the green shaded light filtering through, the thick carpet of pine needles dry and crackly underfoot. Dampness clung in the cold air she breathed. Here the sun never penetrated to warm and give life, only the tops of the trees saw it, and reached up, taller still.

Vanessa stopped walking, and looked upwards, and the trunks went on for ever, and they seemed to close in on her. Everything spun round suddenly and she reached out to touch the nearest tree to steady herself – and realized how empty she was. All she had eaten at dinner had been a few mouthfuls of soup – before she had looked at Cal and known that she loved him. Then she had been unable to take more.

It seemed to be growing darker and colder quite suddenly. Her imagination, of course, but she knew that she didn't want to walk any further. No thoughts could help her. All she had to do now was go away. When she returned to Deanston House she would pack her things ready. There were sounds, faint ones like the rustling of paper far away, a low continual scratch-scratch as of tissue paper being crumpled. When she came out from the trees, she knew what it was. It had started to rain, the soft Highland misty rain. It didn't matter. Vanessa didn't care if she got wet. She lifted her face to the sky and the softness caressed her skin and touched her eyes and lashes so that she had to blink. She walked on, and the ground was more springy as it soaked up the moisture, and she kicked a tiny stone and heard it clatter against a larger pebble.

She reached her car, opened the door and slid in. It started at first turn, throbbed, jerked – then whirred as the wheels refused to move. Frowning, she switched off, then tried again. This time it jerked forward a few inches before the whirring began again, and a dreadful thought occurred to her. She switched off, got out, and looked at the wheels. The back ones were firmly embedded in mud.

'Oh no!' After all that had happened, now this. If only she had thought to look before parking. It was no use standing there getting wetter and wetter. Vanessa looked round for branches or twigs, anything to pack under the rear wheels to give them leverage, but there appeared to be nothing – at least not near by. She knew that if she went back to the wood she would be able to gather armfuls of dry twigs and fir cones. And the sooner the better. It was getting darker now that the rain seemed to be settling in for the night. She didn't relish the idea of fumbling in that dark ghostly wood for twigs.

She set off walking back, more quickly now. There was an urgency, brought by the rain, and the sooner she was away the better. She ran into the first trees and, kneeling, began to scoop up armfuls of twigs and leaves – then suddenly she heard the roar of a car gradually growing louder, as it climbed. A car – coming *here*. For a moment Vanessa stood quite still, listening, wondering if her ears were playing her tricks. But there was no mistake. Every second brought the sound more clearly to her. Very quietly she walked to the edge of the trees and looked towards her car, clearly visible a few hundred yards away. Cal Grayne's Jaguar was pulling to a stop beside it.

She stood there quite still, a host of jumbled emotions crowding through her mind in those few first seconds of startled awareness. What was *he* doing here? Not coincidence, surely, that he had come for a ride here, so soon after her? Was he alone? The last question was answered as she saw him get out and go over to her car and open the door. He leaned in, she saw that, as she also saw that his Jaguar was empty; at least he wasn't with the beautiful Heather. She could not have stood that, she knew. Her handbag was on the front seat. He would be looking at it. Would he open it? Vanessa heard the door slam, and opened her eyes, which she had shut at the thought of him prying through her bag. It was no use standing there. She would have to go out – and anyway, hadn't she been needing help? He would provide it – and scorn too – but she was used to that.

She came out of the trees and began to run towards the two cars. She was prepared for his sarcasm, but she wasn't prepared for his anger. She saw him turn and watch her and as she got nearer he began to walk towards her and his first words left her in no doubt at all about the state of his temper.

'What the bloody *hell* do you think you're playing at?' he demanded.

She stood still, shocked.

'What?'

'I said – what the hell are you playing at?' Green eyes darker with temper, he stood there, big and assured and in a fine old rage – which had the oddest effect on Vanessa. She began to laugh. Perhaps it was sheer tension that brought it on, she didn't know, but the laughter pealed forth until tears ran down her cheeks, and Cal took hold of her arms and shook her.

'Stop it!' he said.

She did so, sobered by the steely quietness of that deep voice. He still held her, and she wondered what he would do if she blurted out: 'I love you, Cal, so please don't touch me, because if you do I shall want to kiss you.' How appalling! She stood there looking at him, her face pale and serious because of the thoughts chasing through her mind, but he didn't know that. His own face softened slightly, and he released her.

'All right,' he said. 'I'm sorry I shouted at you. But just listen a minute. You vanish – after not eating a damned thing at dinner – vanish in your car, God knows where, and that's it, for two hours, not a sign of you, and—' Two hours! It had surely only been five minutes that she had been here – and yet – she stole a quick glance at her watch. It was true. Gone half past nine. She looked at him.

'I can go out for a drive in the evening if I want,' she answered, more calm all of a sudden. It was not to last.

'I don't see why you should get so mad.'

'Mad? Yes, I was. I thought you'd run away—'

The flare of shock widened her eyes, and he gave a cynical, twisted smile. 'I called round to see Laurie—' there was a pause, and she waited, holding her breath because she *knew* what was to come. She *knew*, and there was nothing she could do about it.

'And I asked him if he knew where you were – after all, it was no use going out looking for you if—' a faint shrug, '—you were with him. He went a bit pale – my question had shaken him, I could see that.' Vanessa half turned away, unable to see those eyes, but Cal put a gentle hand on her arm. 'So I got it out of him. You're planning to go—'

'Oh, Laurie!' It was wrenched out of her in despair.

'Don't blame him. I wouldn't have left him until he'd told me—'

'Oh, I bet you're good at that,' she exclaimed bitterly.

'Yes. But he didn't tell me *who* you are – he didn't need to. I already know.'

She thought she might faint. She had to look at him then. 'Does *he* know?' She didn't need to say her grandfather's name. They both knew she didn't mean Laurie.

'No one knows except me.'

'How – how did you find out?' She could scarcely say the words. The world was a suddenly frightening place with nowhere to run, to escape. Even the ground seemed to be moving underfoot, shifting and changing as if there were an earthquake. But Cal seemed unaware of it, so it must be her. She began to shiver helplessly and he took her arm. 'Get in my car.'

'No.' She tried to shake his hand free, but he had a grip of steel.

'Yes. We're not standing here in this damn rain. You're getting soaked. You won't be going anywhere if you get pneumonia.' She was propelled towards his car, the door opened, and she found herself inside. The next moment he was in the driver's seat, passing her her handbag, switching on the heater, and the whirring sound as warm air filled the car came loudly in her ears. She leaned back against the seat exhausted, heard him say something, but not taking the words in until a bundle of paper handkerchiefs was thrust into her hand.

'Rub your face and hair. Go on, do as you're told. Now.' Perhaps it was easier to do just that, rather than argue.

'How did I find out?' He was watching her as she rubbed her face, then started dabbing at her long hair. 'Take your coat off, Vanessa, the car's warm enough now.'

She obediently leaned forward to pull her arms out of the sleeves of her jacket, and he took hold of it and eased it off, then flung it on the back seat.

'I guessed. I was uneasy about you right from the beginning. There was something odd, but I didn't know what it was — until last night.' Vanessa didn't speak. He would tell her in his own good time. Maybe he was even enjoying himself — she didn't know or care any more. She felt drained of all strength.

'I saw a photo of Andrew Maclean's son last night at Heather's house. She didn't know. She'd got an old box of excruciatingly boring holiday snaps out for me to see one of her taken with some minor Royal when she was a child—' he paused for a moment. 'While she was riffling through, I saw the one of Andrew taken years ago with his son as a boy. What it was doing there I didn't ask. I pocketed it,' he added with a note of quiet humour. 'I'm quite good at that if I want to be. Want to see it?'

'No.'

'I think you should. The likeness is there, well defined. I'm only surprised your — grandfather hadn't spotted it.'

She turned on him then, because she couldn't bear it any more. 'All right. What are you going to do?'

'Do?' His eyes narrowed. 'Me? Nothing.'

Her mouth twisted with the effort not to cry out. 'Don't give me that. Aren't you pleased with yourself?' She swallowed hard, determined not to show weakness to *him*. 'It's what you've been waiting for, isn't it? Well, go on, tell him. I d-don't care.'

'I think you do,' he said quietly. 'In fact I'd lay odds on it. Now, I'm going to get you home before you're ill.'

'My car's stuck—'

'I know.' He switched on the engine. 'But you're not fit to drive anywhere. I'll come back for it with Laurie—'

'He hates you!' she burst out. Anything to delay leaving.

'Does he?' he seemed almost amused. 'Did he tell you why?'

'Yes.'

'What did he say?'

'I'm not discussing it. I'm not discussing anything with *you*.'

173

'If he told you about his sister I'll bet he coloured it a bit. So I'll tell you my side – then it's up to you to decide who to believe. And I don't give a damn either way, I assure you.' He switched off the engine again. 'It's quite simple, although it'll make me sound conceited, but it happens to be the truth. She took a fancy to me. Quite a nice-looking girl, only I didn't fancy her, which annoyed her considerably, because between you and me she's a spoilt little hussy. So she told her brother that I'd tried to seduce her – I told you this would make me sound conceited – and he got me one night in the gardens and tried to beat hell out of me. I didn't even know what I was supposed to have *done* – only unfortunately for him I knew a bit too much judo and he came off worse. I let him down lightly – I mean I didn't actually bash him up, only defended myself, and got it out of him what crime I was supposed to have committed. He didn't believe me when I assured him I'd never even touched the girl – and his pride was badly dented too, I suppose, because I found out since that he was an amateur boxing champion for this area. So that's why he dislikes me. Incidentally, his sister took off soon after for the brighter lights of Aberdeen, where no doubt she'll be better appreciated. And that's *my* story.'

He switched on the engine, decisively, and Vanessa sat quite still. She believed him. It had helped her for a moment to forget the other overwhelming story he had told her about herself. That could have been why he had done it. She looked at him as he steered the car on to the track that led to the road. She felt extremely confused. How could you love and hate someone at the same moment? It should be impossible, and yet that was precisely how she felt. She sat very quiet, exhausted beyond words, her head against the warm comfortable headrest to the seat, a faint sick hunger and emptiness inside her. Cal had said he intended doing nothing with his knowledge of her identity, and she believed that he spoke the truth. The thought of the letter waiting in her bedroom came to her. She knew that in the morning, early, she would leave.

Very casually she asked: 'Will you come back for my car tonight? Only it's not locked.'

'I know. It's safe enough there.' He gave her a swift sidelong glance. 'But I'll come back tonight, don't worry.'

'Thank you.' There was nothing more to say, except one thing. She must have the keys to drive away in the morning. 'Would you leave the keys in that bowl in the hall when you come back, in case I'm asleep?'

'If you like. I won't lose them.' She couldn't tell him that that wasn't what she was concerned about, so she said nothing, and the rest of the journey passed in silence.

Cal drove to the front of the house and came round to open her door for her. 'In you go. I'll get Mrs. Banks to fetch you up some supper after I've told your — Mr. Maclean that you're safely back. I'll explain that your car was stuck and you were trying to shift it yourself.' She looked at him as they went up the steps to the porch. Something must have shown in her eyes, for he added softly: 'And that's all I'm going to tell him. The rest is up to you, Vanessa.' The door opened, they went in, and Vanessa crossed the hall and went slowly up the stairs. She had to hold tight to the banister rail.

It was an effort to undress and wash and climb in

between warm sheets. She dared not chance packing now and being caught by Mrs. Banks; she would do it later, when she had eaten. For Vanessa knew she must eat if only to give her strength to drive away in the morning.

She lay there, and sleep had nearly overtaken her when there was a knock on the door. Vanessa struggled to sit up, and called out: 'Come in.'

It wasn't Mrs. Banks, it was Cal with a tray. Confused, she pulled the sheet up round her shoulders, and stared at him in alarm.

'It's all right, I'm not looking.' A faint smile touched his mouth. 'Mrs. Banks blasted me halfway out of her kitchen. She was doing a special cake for tomorrow, so I volunteered to bring this up.' He came forward. The tray held soup, toast, apple pie with a dollop of thick cream, and the inevitable pot of coffee. 'Is it enough?'

'Plenty, thank you. I didn't expect—' she faltered, blinking back tears of weakness. 'Th-thank you for bringing it up.'

He put the tray on her knee, carefully, and looked at her, and it seemed as if he was about to say something. Then he turned and went to the door. He paused just before closing it behind him. 'Good night, Vanessa,' he said.

'Good night.' Then, when he had closed the door, she added softly: 'And good-bye.' That was it. She would not see him again. She took a deep breath and began the soup.

Sleep, when it came at last, was disturbed and restless, with frightening dreams that woke Vanessa up several times. She sat up after a particularly vivid one in which she was lost in a vast forest of huge trees, and someone was chasing her. She couldn't see who it was, only hear her name being called over and over: 'Vanessa!' The whole atmosphere of the dream had been sad and lost, and she knew that she wouldn't get to sleep again so easily, so she crept out of bed to see the clock, fearful to switch on the light for more than a second or two, lest it was noticed. It was nearly five. She looked at the warm bed, sheets tumbled with the restlessness that had taken her in its grip. If she fell asleep again, it might be eight when she woke, too late for escape. It must be now.

Her cases were packed, hidden in the bathroom, ready and waiting. All she had to do was dress, put her nightie in a case, collect her keys, and go. And put out the letter on the tray; that was the one final task she must not forget. Very quietly and quickly she pulled on the warm blue trews and sweater she had left out the previous night. She put the letter on the tray, a horrible feeling inside her as she did so. An awful sad, lost sensation, for it represented the final step, the very last step of a sad journey.

She crept quietly down the stairs carrying her cases. She had to put one down in the hall to pick the keys from out of the bowl. Cal had kept his word, gone back for her car and left the keys where she had asked.

Vanessa blinked back sudden tears and went to open the door. It was never bolted, not even at night, a fact which had surprised her somewhat on her arrival. She was grateful for the fact now, for the door swung open easily for her. She shut it carefully after her, picked up her cases, and went down the steps. Cottonwool drifts of mist lay heavily over the grass, and the air she breathed was damp and very cold. She shivered, and looked back at the house. It slept, as did the people within.

She turned away and began walking quickly towards the garage. Her footsteps crunched on the gravel, so she stepped on the grass verge, and stayed on that until she reached the last few yards across. Still nothing stirred. Even the kitchen blinds were down, no lights behind them.

Vanessa put her cases on the front passenger seat, closed her door quietly and switched on the engine. It whirred a few times, but that was all. Frowning, she tried again. Surely it wasn't so cold outside? The second time there was the same result.

'Damn, damn!' she muttered. Of all times for this to happen! She pulled the bonnet catch to check that everything was all right, got out, careful to leave her door ajar – the less noise she made, the better – and lifted the bonnet and peered inside the engine, not even sure what she was looking for, yet with a small nagging unease at the back of her mind. She had a slight knowledge of engines, but that was all. Everything seemed as it should be.

She was about to press the bonnet down and go back and try again when she saw that one of the clips from the distributor cap was hanging loose. The small nagging unease crystallized into sharp suspicion as she leaned over and unclipped the other one, and lifted the cap. The rotor arm was missing from inside – and she knew straightaway who had taken it. Cal. Of course! It had happened once before, as a joke after a party. Someone had taken the rotor arm from her car so that she would let him take her home. She had fallen for it that time, and the would-be suitor had confessed his 'crime' over a candlelit dinner the following night, and Vanessa had been amused at the ploy. But not now. There was nothing amusing in this situation.

She closed the bonnet gently and ran out of the garage back to the house. So he had taken the rotor arm. She intended to go and get it back from him. He would not have thrown it away. The most likely thing would be that he would have it in his room. Why, but why? The question hammered in her brain as she ran along the damp grass verge, the mist swirling and dispersing around her as she went, and then going back to where it had been. Two baby rabbits lolloped away, surprised, but she didn't even notice. She was too upset. The door clicked open and she pushed it shut and ran up the stairs. Anger was taking the place of alarm now, a warm tide surging through her, lending colour to her cheeks and fire to her eyes. The arrogance of the man to do such a thing! How *dare* he!

She reached his bedroom door and her momentum faltered, just for a second – then she pushed the door open and went in.

Cal lay fast alseep in bed, a dark shape under the bedclothes. The curtains were drawn back, windows wide open, and early light and cold air filtered in. One arm outflung, he lay on his side, quite still, his breathing deep and steady.

On the bedside table was an alarm clock, wallet, car keys and a book. Vanessa looked at them, her breathing swift and shallow as she contemplated what she had to do now. Then she leaned forward and shook him.

Instantly he woke, eyes open, looking at her, his voice yet blurred with sleep as he said: 'What's up?'

'Where is it?' she demanded.

He passed a hand over his face and struggled to sit

179

up, peered at the clock, said: 'Good God, do you know what time it is?'

'Yes. Where's the rotor arm from my car?'

'Ah!' A long-drawn-out sound, explicit in the understanding it held. 'Ah – *that*.'

'Yes, that.' Her fists clenched and unclenched involuntarily. She was having to restrain herself from hitting him hard. It would not do her any good if she did. He would certainly give her nothing then. She had to fight for calm, to enable her to say: 'Please may I have it?'

He was fully awake now, and aware, and he sat up properly, looked at her, and shook his head. 'No.'

'W-why not?'

'Because then you'll run away—'

'What's it to do with *you*?' she demanded angrily.

'Plenty. I have no intention of letting you sneak out of here like—'

'Go to hell!' She half turned away, to give her time to fight the treacherous temper rising fast within her. Then she saw again his car keys on the table. Keys to start the Jaguar. She snatched them up before she had time to think what she was doing, for it would come under the heading of theft, wouldn't it? – but she didn't care. It was his fault. 'Then I'll take your car,' she said. 'Good-bye. I'll write and tell you where to collect it.' She turned and ran out of the room. Quickly – down the stairs, across the hall – faster – he wasn't fully awake, please don't let him be, she prayed silently. Every second counted. Down the steps, along the path, no use trying to keep her footsteps silent on the grass; it was too late for that now – too late.

Fear and desperation lent wings to her feet and she

sped along. There *would* be time. Her cases – she must put her cases in the Jaguar. It had been next to her Cortina in the garage, and the doors were open, all she had to do was ... She reached the darkness of the garage, wrenched open her door to remove the cases, bent to lift them again, and looked up as the shadow fell on her, and Cal stood there, barefoot, dressed in faded jeans and blue pyjama top. He took a deep breath.

'You certainly can run,' he said.

She straightened up, too incensed now to bother about anything except the one desire paramount – to escape from him. 'Get out of my way,' she said, and picked up her cases.

'You've got to be joking. Put them down. Fun and games over, love. Come on back to the house – and calm down.' He took the cases from her, and the fact that he'd called her love didn't register until later. She only saw his impudent hands reaching out, taking her cases from her, and the pent-up anger inside her finally boiled over. She struck out blindly at him with both hands, and he laughed, dropped her cases and held her so that she was helpless.

'I warned you what would happen if you tried to hit me,' he said, almost amused, and then he kissed her.

He kissed her, and it seemed that time had stopped, that the world had ceased spinning, and that there were only the two of them in the whole universe. Then it was over, and they drew apart, and the very air seemed to tremble as they looked at one another. Cal's face was dark in the shadowy confines of that garage, and he spoke softly, as if fearful to break the spell.

'Vanessa,' he said. 'Oh, Vanessa. What am I to do with you?'

Her voice shook. 'Let me go, Cal. Let me go away now.'

'No,' it was a gentle whisper. 'Not now – not ever. Here, get in the Jag, you're shaking.' This time she could not resist him. He slid in beside her and switched on the heater, and put his arms round her straightaway. 'Don't fight me, Vanessa,' he said. 'Don't struggle. I can't bear it.'

'I don't – I don't know what you're talking about,' she answered, her heart beating suffocatingly fast. 'We don't – I hate you and you hate me.'

'No, I don't,' he said, and ran his finger gently down her cheek. 'You've always had the power to disturb me more than you know – but I didn't realize why until last night when I thought you'd run away. God! You don't know how I felt when Laurie said that, and I thought you'd gone. Then I knew. I knew how I felt about you – and I know how you feel about me. Don't try and deny it. I *know*.'

'You're a conceited swine,' she said, her voice so faint that it was almost a whisper. But he heard, and laughed.

'Conceited swine! I like that – yes, I like that. In fact, I don't give a damn what you call me. I saw it in your eyes last night. You can't hide *that*, Vanessa.'

Her heart was bursting now. She moved just a few inches so that she could look into his eyes, and saw the love in them, and reached up to touch his face.

'Oh, Cal, help me. I'm running away because – because—' this was going to be difficult. The time for lies and deception was over. There could be no more of that – not with him. Not now. She swallowed, faltered, then went on: 'I came here to see what he – my grandfather was like. I hated him, because my father had told me how cruel he had been. I came to see him – I knew he was looking for his granddaughter, and I was going to get him to like m-me, and then – g-go away—'

'Don't. You don't need—'

'Yes, I *do*,' she whispered fiercely. 'Because I hate myself – that's why I'm running away – that's why you'll hate me when I've finished telling you. I met him – and I began to like him—' she stopped and put her head in her hands, and the tears she had sworn not to shed again flowed freely now. Her body shook. She heard Cal's groan, felt his hand on the back of her neck, stroking gently, and it was all too much to bear. Helplessly she turned and buried her face against his chest. He put his arms round her, and cradled her gently, as he would have a child, and murmured softly:

'Don't cry, my love, please don't cry.'

'I c-can't help it.'

'*Listen*, Vanessa,' he took a deep gulping breath, then was silent, because there was an intensity in his words that made her stop. 'Listen. He *needs* you. Can't you see that? He needs you desperately. Your running away would be unbearably cruel. You're going to stay, Vanessa, if I have to use force – and I will. You're going to stay, and we're going to see your grandfather, you and I together, and tell him—'

'No,' a muffled answer, but he heard it.

'Yes! I love you, dammit. I'm not going to let you go now.'

She leaned back. 'What?'

'I said I love you. Are you blind? Can't you tell?'

'You – but what about Heather?'

'Heather? She'd drive me mad in six months. All that

girl is interested in is herself and her looks. Sure, she's good company – in small doses – but you, my dark beauty, knock her into a cocked hat without even trying.'

'Oh.' She couldn't have said more if she had tried.

'And so,' he went on, and his arms tightened about her fractionally, as if making sure that she couldn't get away even if she wanted to – but she didn't, of course – and his touch was all she had ever wanted it to be. 'You're not going away from *me* – unless you want me to follow wherever you go, and catch you.'

'No,' she took a deep shuddering breath. 'No, I knew I loved you last night – at dinner.' She had to smile at the memory. 'Over the soup, to be precise. I looked at you – and wham! It hit me just like that.'

'My God! Is *that* why you couldn't eat?' He began to laugh softly. 'Do I have that effect on you?'

Her smile broadened slightly. 'I suppose so,' she admitted softly. 'Oh, Cal. How – why?'

He didn't need to ask what she meant. 'Because, my little idiot, some things are meant, that's why. You remember that day I came into the library and saw Laurie's face, and knew he'd kissed you. I had to forcibly restrain myself from giving him a good hiding then. Couldn't understand it then – fool that I was. Then gradually this feeling grew, and I fought it, because I knew you were phoney – didn't know exactly why, not then – but the suspicion was growing all the time, together with this terrific feeling of wanting to kiss you at the same time. I nearly did, once, in the judo lesson. You never knew. That's one thing judo teaches you, a certain measure of self-discipline – and by golly, I needed it that day.'

'I was a pig to you, wasn't I?' she asked softly.

'How can I agree with that? I guess I was pretty ghastly to you, my sweet. But it's all over now. Now we know, I mean. Oh, Vanessa, my love, am I glad I took that blasted rotor arm out!'

'Oh yes. Where is it anyway?' she demanded, but the sparkle in her eyes was not one of anger now.

'Hidden in a tool box at the back of the garage where you'd never have found it. I had this feeling you'd try to leave, and I wanted to make sure you didn't. I never expected you to come storming up to my room, though. Wow! What a temper!'

'I'm sorry, love,' she murmured.

'You'd better be. There'll be none of that when we're married.'

'Oh!'

'Is that all you can say?'

'Yes. Till I get my breath back. I wasn't sure if I heard—'

'You did. Will you, Vanessa? Marry me, I mean?'

'Yes. Oh yes!'

'Come on, love.' He squinted at his watch. 'God, nearly six! Listen, let's creep into the kitchen and make ourselves a cup of tea or something. Mrs Banks won't be up till seven.'

'All right.' And there was something else she had to say. Better now, before they left the warm dark car.

'Cal?'

'Yes?'

'I want to see my grandfather alone. Please. I must tell him myself.'

'You're sure?'

'Yes. I must do it by myself. You do understand,

don't you?'

He smiled at her as they walked out, and the mist had magically cleared, and his face, and eyes, were full of love. 'Yes, my darling, I understand. But I'll be waiting for you. And – don't worry. Just tell him in your own sweet way. He'll understand.'

'I hope so.' She closed her eyes. 'I left him a letter. It was difficult to write. But now I'm glad you stopped me going. You'll never know how glad.'

'No?' his arm tightened around her, and he pointed. 'See that hill over there?'

Vanessa looked at the bleak shape towering in the distance, its peak snow-patched. 'I'll love you as long as the snow stays on that hill,' he told her, and she smiled.

'It never goes away; it's there for ever.'

'Yes,' he said. And kissed her.

Best Seller Romances

Next month's best loved romances

Mills & Boon Best Seller Romances are the love stories that have proved particularly popular with our readers. These are the titles to look out for next month.

STRANGE ADVENTURE Sara Craven
SWEET PROMISE Janet Dailey
JUNGLE OF DESIRE Flora Kidd
THE UNWILLING BRIDEGROOM Roberta Leigh
WILD ENCHANTRESS Anne Mather
THE BURNING SANDS Violet Winspear

Buy them from your usual paperback stockist, or write to: Mills & Boon Reader Service, P.O. Box 236, Thornton Rd, Croydon, Surrey CR9 3RU, England. Readers in South Africa-write to: Mills & Boon Reader Service of Southern Africa, Private Bag X3010, Randburg, 2125.

Mills & Boon
the rose of romance

Doctor Nurse Romances

Romance in the wide world of medicine

Amongst the intense emotional pressures of modern medical life, doctors and nurses often find romance. Read about their lives and loves in the three fascinating Doctor Nurse romances, available this month.

HOSPITAL ACROSS THE BRIDGE
Lisa Cooper

BACHELOR DOCTOR
Sonia Deane

NEW SURGEON AT ST LUCIAN'S
Elizabeth Houghton

Mills & Boon
the rose of romance

ROMANCE

Variety is the spice of romance

Each month, Mills & Boon publish new romances. New stories about people falling in love. A world of variety in romance – from the best writers in the romantic world. Choose from these titles in December.

WEDDING OF THE YEAR Anne Weale
A PASSIONATE AFFAIR Anne Mather
COUNTERFEIT BRIDE Sara Craven
THIS TIME IS FOR EVER Sheila Strutt
PASSIONATE INTRUDER Lilian Peake
A DREAM CAME TRUE Betty Neels
THE MAN SHE MARRIED Violet Winspear
BOUGHT WITH HIS NAME Penny Jordan
MAN FROM THE KIMBERLEYS Margaret Pargeter
HANDMAID TO MIDAS Jane Arbor
DEVIL IN DISGUISE Jessica Steele
MELT A FROZEN HEART Lindsay Armstrong

On sale where you buy paperbacks. If you require further information or have any difficulty obtaining them, write to: Mills & Boon Reader Service, PO Box 236, Thornton Road, Croydon, Surrey CR9 3RU, England.

Mills & Boon
the rose of romance

Best Seller Romances

Romances you have loved

Mills & Boon Best Seller Romances are the love stories that have proved particularly popular with our readers. They really are "back by popular demand." These are the other titles to look out for this month.

ERRANT BRIDE
by Elizabeth Ashton

Antoine de Mericourt was going to turn Sylvie into a great star of the ballet – which was why he had married her, just to ensure that no romantic distractions would interfere with her career. He had no intention of allowing the marriage to become a real one – but what about Sylvie's feelings?

A KISS FROM SATAN
by Anne Hampson

'Place your hand on a woman's heart and she's yours instantly,' said the arrogant Greek Julius Spiridon. Gale, embittered after being let down by the man she loved, had vowed never to let a man touch her heart again. So she was absolutely determined to fight the attraction she so unwillingly felt for Julius...

Mills & Boon

TOO YOUNG TO LOVE
by Roberta Leigh

Sara was only eighteen when she fell in love with Gavin Baxter – which was perhaps the reason why her stepmother had so easily made mischief and wrecked the affair. Now Sara was older and Gavin had come back into her life. Was she mature enough now to win his love a second time?

DARK VENETIAN
by Anne Mather

Emma ought to have known that her stepmother Celeste never did anything except for selfish reasons, and even a holiday in a Venetian *palazzo* could not compensate her for the heartache she was to suffer. Celeste wanted to add a title to her wealth – but did it *have* to be Count Vidal Cesare, the man Emma herself loved?

RIDE A BLACK HORSE
by Margaret Pargeter

The advertisement for a Girl Friday seemed just the job Jane was looking for – the chance to work in the country and train for a riding school of her own. The owner Karl Grierson, was *not* quite what Jane had been looking for, though!

the rose of romance

How to join in a whole new world of romance

It's very easy to subscribe to the Mills & Boon Reader Service. As a regular reader, you can enjoy a whole range of special benefits. Bargain offers. Big cash savings. Your own free Reader Service newsletter, packed with knitting patterns, recipes, competitions, and exclusive book offers.

We send you the very latest titles each month, postage and packing free – no hidden extra charges. There's absolutely no commitment – you receive books for only as long as you want.

We'll send you details. Simply send the coupon – or drop us a line for details about the Mills & Boon Reader Service Subscription Scheme.

Post to: Mills & Boon Reader Service, P.O. Box 236, Thornton Road, Croydon, Surrey CR9 3RU, England.
*Please note: READERS IN SOUTH AFRICA please write to: Mills & Boon Reader Service of Southern Africa, Private Bag X3010, Randburg 2125, S. Africa.

Please send me details of the Mills & Boon Subscription Scheme.
NAME (Mrs/Miss) _____ EP3
ADDRESS _____
_____
COUNTY/COUNTRY _____ POST/ZIP CODE _____
BLOCK LETTERS, PLEASE

Mills & Boon
the rose of romance